CHANGING FORTUNES

Gabriel Ellison

Gadsden Publishers
Lusaka

Gadsden Publishers

PO Box 32581, Lusaka, Zambia

Cover Photograph - Punish Chidembo

ISBN 978-9982-240-95-6

Printed by Lightening Source UK Ltd

Chapter 1

When her father had not returned to the house by the time the moon had risen and the vast township had fallen quiet, apart from the incessant throb of the disco bar and a few still active radios, Malele felt a cold fear creep over her. Her mother muttered about drunken husbands and wasted suppers, unworried by her husband's absence, but Malele shivered and could not sleep on the hard bed mat.

Her mother had retired to her room, angry at his absence. Mother was often angry, her mouth drooping at the corners and her frown deepening between her brows. She was resentful of their poverty and longed to return to the village where she had grown up. In her mind the village had none of the squalor and noise of the township, and was bathed in tranquillity. Malele had expected so much when she had been taken there for a fleeting visit and the disappointment of the shabby huts, the coarse scratchy grass and the clinging dust made her question her mother's dreams and complain to her father. As always, he smiled and answered gently.

'That is her dream, my child. Let people have their dreams. She would not like to stay there, but one needs a place to go to in one's mind when things are hard at home.'

'How can that help?' Malele asked. 'Things are still the same in real life.'

'You will learn one day. What it is to be young!'

Malele thought about her father, her gentle, resolute father who tried to fire his child with educational ambition and a desire to improve her lifestyle. He was employed as a day guard with a factory and his salary was inadequate for the needs of his family. But they managed, skimping on essentials so that Malele could go to school. It was her father who protected Malele from the bitterness of her mother.

'The schooling is better here in town,' he told his wife.

'And I have a job although it doesn't pay much. Some day things will improve, and in the meantime we are managing.'

'I am fed up with just managing,' said Jess Simonga.

Malele remembered the day that the conversation took place and how James, her father, tried to coax his wife into a better humour. She loved her father more than her mother, who was inclined to complain about everything.

An owl hooted softly in the trees, far off at the edge of the compound. Malele heard it and tried not to listen. Owls were bad omens. Her grandmother had told her so many tales about the evil owls that she feared them and believed in their evil. She lay, half dreaming, listening for her father until the thin sound of the roosters crowing showed that the morning was breaking and it would soon be light. Malele stood up and dressed quietly, then crept out into the faint light. The sun was only a pink hue behind the trees and the dew soaked her feet as she moved over the dry grass to the communal tap. The water was cold and stung her face as she splashed it onto her skin. Other people were moving about, radios started up in the distance and the sun now showed the colour of blood behind the trees. She knew that he had not returned. She would have heard him.

'He has not come back.' Her mother joined her at the tap, pulling her chitenge cloth tighter round her waist. 'Too drunk I suppose.'

Malele could hear the uncertainty in her voice. He had never stayed out all night before.

'Too drunk. I am sure that is all it is, Malele. Men are like that. Some stay with their girlfriends but not your father. I do not believe that he has another woman. It can only be the beer.' She paused, then her anger returned and she went on, 'Drunken beast. All that money wasted and there is so little for us. How can he? He was not like that when we married. Oh no,

4

he was a lad from the village who was ambitious and who had ideas of getting rich in the town, so off we went. We should have stayed in the village where he had cattle and land, but no, he thought that the town was the place to be.'

'Hush, amai. Perhaps he has become ill or something. If he was drunk, so drunk that he could not walk, his friends would have helped him and brought him home.' Malele caught her mother by the hand. 'Come, amai. I will go and find where he is. It is light and you must stay here with the others. I will go quickly and find him. How lucky that there is no school today.'

She walked along the road towards the tavern, brittle with anxiety. Whenever an acquaintance passed, Malele asked if they had seen her father as he had not come home. They shook their heads and she did not linger to talk. There were few people about as it was Sunday and for most, a day off work.

The tavern was closed and shabby in the weak sunlight, the paint peeling scabrously off the walls and the red Coca Cola sign disfigured by graffiti. A weary looking man came out of the back door, tossing the dirty water out of his bucket into the dust. He ignored the girl until she spoke.

'Have you seen my father, James Simonga? He didn't come home last night.'

The man paused for a moment. 'He was drinking here last night with some others after work. I didn't see him leave but there were many people and we closed very late. He must have gone as there is no one here now except me. Probably slept in the ditch, mama. Many men fail to get home after drinking, or perhaps he went home with some girl. Men do that too as you will find out. Not so long now.' He laughed and spat into the dust, his eyes moving over her body. 'A girl not much older than you perhaps?'

'He has no girlfriend. I know that. He hasn't come home and we are worried about him. He has never done that before.'

5

'Always a first time. Who knows, perhaps the police picked him up, but I doubt if they would bother ... too many drunks on a Saturday so unless he did something very bad they would have looked away.'

'He could have had an accident?' Malele felt the cold panic sweep over her.

'Could have. Go and ask at the police post if you are worried, but my bet is that he is in a nice warm bed with a girl.'

Malele hated him silently and turned away towards the distant police post. There, the sleepy constable on duty assured her that there were no James Simongas in the cells and even allowed her to peer through the bars into the semi-darkness. Several people were sitting on the floor, but not her father. She thanked the constable and stood wondering what to do. The dust was caught up by the wind and spun round her. She closed her eyes against the stinging grains, then, as the wind slackened she could see a man running down the road, waving his arms and shouting something. He passed her and went into the police post. Malele turned to go back along the road, but the police constable burst out of the small building followed by the man.

'There is a body in the ditch by the crossroads,' he said.

Malele followed at a distance, full of a terrible fear that it was her father who lay in the ditch. A small crowd of people had gathered at the crossroads and were looking down into the drain that bordered the road. Malele joined them. The grass was rank and weeds straggled along the verge. She pushed forward, her heart hammering so loudly that she expected the others to hear it. She forced herself to stand at the edge of the ditch, then glanced down, not wanting to see what was there. Lying in the shadows was the familiar figure of her father, his shirt awry and his face downwards. Blood had pooled round his head and had dried into a black shadow. His arms spread up the narrowness of the earth trench but his legs were straight and one shoe had come off and lay at a small distance. Malele screamed and slid down into the ditch where the police constable was bending over the body. He looked up and caught her by the arm.

'Don't touch him, sister. Get back and out of the way. Is this your father?'

'Yes.' Malele had tears streaming down her face. 'Is he dead?'

She felt strange and impersonal. People were talking above her on the verge, curious and uninvolved.

'Yes, he is dead. I am sorry, sister. We will have to leave him where he is until the CID come. Someone must have hit him on the head. You can see that all the back of his head is broken. It must have been a very hard blow. Come, wait with all the others while I go and call for help.'

He helped her out of the ditch and left her with a motherly-looking woman. 'I won't be long. Wait here and when I come back you can give me the particulars of your father.'

More people had arrived, talking and exclaiming. A second constable arrived and chased everyone back.

'Keep away. You can see that the man is dead and we are waiting for the CID. Get back everyone. You don't need to see what is there in the ditch. The man is the father of this girl and is nothing to do with you.'

Malele broke free of the woman's arms and started running down the road towards her home.

'Must fetch amai,' she shouted as she ran, ignoring the crowd and pushing past anyone who stood in her way. She ran blindly, intent on reaching home and amai, but when she neared the house she stopped and then went forward slowly, hating to bring the terrible news and wondering how to break it. Her mother was cooking over a small fire and looked up as Malele approached.

'What is it?' The look on Malele's face was a portent of bad news. 'What has happened?' She caught the girl by the arm.

'Amai, he is dead. Killed and lying in a ditch. The police are there.'

Malele buried her face in her mother's arms, willing her to take over the whole situation and to be the strong one, but her mother began to wail and to cling to Malele as though the girl was their strength.

'Dead? How can that be? Oh, what will become of us now? Now we will have no one and nothing.'

Malele tried to gather her energy. 'Hush, amai. We must go to the place quickly and see what is happening.' She was holding her mother tightly. A passing friend came hurrying to them, hearing the wailing and starting her own cries although she did not know what was wrong. Malele turned on her.

'Be quiet. My father is dead and amai and I have to go to where he is. We will come back soon.' She spoke roughly, caught up in her own fear. Suddenly she seemed to be the one in charge and she hated the responsibility.

The wailing had attracted some of the neighbours. Mrs Mboloma, a stout motherly woman who lived nearby came hurrying to see what had happened. Malele was sobbing again, but as her mother was clinging onto her arm she had to be the one in charge. Quickly she told Mrs Mboloma the news and the three hurried off, amai still wailing and weeping.

By the time they reached the ditch the CID had arrived and were examining the body. The police van stood ready to take it to the mortuary. Malele watched silently as her father was lifted out of the ditch onto a stretcher and placed in the police van. Her mother tried to go forward to the stretcher but was held back.

'Come with me to the station,' one of the policemen said.

'You can do nothing for the man and we will have to get a statement from you. I understand that your husband did not come home last night?'

He looked from the wailing woman to Malele for an answer. The girl nodded and Mrs Mboloma took amai's arm as they followed the policeman.

'We have had so much of this sort of thing,' he said conversationally. 'Was it payday?'

'Yes,' Malele whispered.

'Robbery most likely as he had nothing in his pockets. We do our best to find the criminal but we seldom do. Did he have any enemies?'

'I don't know. I don't think so. Amai may know, but she is too upset to think.'

It was Malele who gave most of the statement to the police. Her mother clung to her and had to be prompted to answer when Malele could not. It was late morning when they returned to the house and began the sad task of sending messages to James Simonga's relatives. Most of them lived in Chipata, but one cousin who worked in town was contacted and asked to phone his father.

'They will take everything,' amai said. 'When the relatives come they will take all we have and I shall have to go with his brother. At least that will be back to the village.'

'But now the relatives aren't allowed to take our things,' Malele said. 'Amai, you know that. We saw it in the newspapers. Things have changed and you won't have to go with my father's brother. The government has changed all that.'

'So they say, but nothing has changed. We will all go back to the village. My family is there too and there is nothing here for us anyway.'

'But amai, what about school? I must go to school otherwise I will not be able to get a job later. Please amai, let me go to school.'

'School? And where is the money coming from for school? There are the three of you to think about and no money. Don't imagine that your relatives have money for you.

They have their own families and whatever we get will be a kindness on their part. You have had some schooling so you are luckier than the other two who have only just started.'

Malele was silent. The terrible events of the day seemed to be like a thick blanket around her. Her whole life was about to change and things would never be the same again. For a moment she longed to be a little girl again, to be looked after and to have no responsibilities, but that was a dream. Now she had to be strong.

Chapter 2

Malele's life changed. There was no clue as to who had killed her father and eventually the police released his body for burial. His few relatives came to the house and after the funeral started to claim his possessions. Amai sat mutely, watching her husband's brothers taking what little there was. It was part of the tradition she told Malele when the girl protested that it was no longer the custom and that the government had forbidden it.

'You are a child,' amai said, her eyes dull. 'This is what happens and there is nothing that I can do to stop it. I will go back to the village with your uncle and you will come with me. There we will find a new life.'

'I won't go to the village,' Malele shouted. 'I want to stay here. I want to go to school here, not to some village school which teaches nothing.'

'Be quiet, child. Who is going to pay for your schooling may I ask? There is no money and the family has none either. Where are you to live if I am gone and there is no money for rent? At least in the village we will have family to help us. There is nothing here.'

'You don't want to stay here anyway. You have always wanted to go back to the village,' Malele said bitterly. 'And now it will happen just as you wanted.'

'It is how things are. I will go and you will come too. It is what your father would have expected, and his brother, Silas, will take all of us back.'

'He has taken almost all our things,' said Malele bitterly.

'All the things that my father bought for us. We have nothing now.'

'Be quiet, child. I have told you that this is how things are, so stop making a fuss. The village is a good place for us and my family are there.'

'You just do what Silas tells you to.' Malele felt the tears running down her cheeks. Her mother put her arms round the girl.

'Malele, things will work out. You have been so strong, don't weaken now. We have no money so we have to go. The people who employed your father have paid what they owe, but that is all.'

They went on the bus. Eight hours of jolting over the potholed roads, their meagre belongings tied on the bus roof. Silas went with them. Amai was sullen and angry during the bus ride, but as they neared the village she brightened and started talking about the family there, trying to make Malele familiar with the village. Silas said little. He was kindly enough, but they were only adding to his already large family responsibilities and he was happy to let them go to amai's parents.

'I hate it here,' Malele complained. 'Back at home I had friends and there was plenty to do. Here no one knows anything about life in a city and all they think about is the village.'

'That is not a bad thing,' said amai crossly. 'I am tired of your complaints. Be thankful that we have somewhere to stay and that there is family here. City life! If your father had stayed in the village we would have had cattle and land, but no, he would go to the city and said that he would make his fortune there. So what happens? He gets killed and we have nothing. That is city life for you.'

'But I need to go to a proper school,' Malele pleaded. 'I want to learn and when I finish school I want to be able to earn a good salary. Amai, you know that, and once I have money I will take care of you.'

'That is a nice dream. As far as school goes, Silas says that he will pay for you to go the basic school here. That will see you to Grade Nine, and that is enough for a village girl. A woman should settle down and marry when she is old enough, not have fancy ideas about competing with the men. That is most of the trouble with life in the city. The young women don't think about our tradition and so many end up on the streets.'

'Amai, you don't understand. You are so old-fashioned and you live in the past. Women must compete with the men and learn to be equal. The school here is very poor and I won't learn much. Couldn't I go back to Lusaka and stay with friends and go to school?'

'Malele, just stop to think for a moment. We have no relatives in Lusaka and no friends who could afford to have you there. The school might take you back if your place hasn't been filled, but the whole idea is silly and shows what a child you are. You either go to the school here and make the best of it or you leave school and help in the home. There is plenty to do, what with the fields and so on, and if you think you are so clever that they can teach you nothing here, just don't waste the money on school.'

'You like the village and you just don't understand,' Malele cried.

Malele went to the small basic school and became part of the village life. The school had few books and the buildings were shabby. At first she hated the place, resenting having to be there, but she was determined to learn all she could.

'Make friends with the other girls,' Amai urged. 'It is stupid to think that you are superior, and they don't like it either. Come on, child, make the best of things. You can't change anything.'

'I don't think I am superior but we have nothing in common and they talk about the village and the life here and I want to be in a city. That is the difference. I like them all right, but we are different. That's all.'

Amai laughed. 'You are the same, and it is time that you

13

decided to settle down and accept this life and forget the town ideas. I know both worlds and this is far better.'

'Maybe for you but not for me.' Malele tossed her head.

'One day I will go back to town.'

'When you are old enough you can. In the meantime stop being difficult and be happy.'

'How can I be happy here?'

It was her grandmother who helped her the most. Esnart, old and with the darkness of her eyes blurred by a blue shadow, felt sorry for the girl and knew that her sharp-tongued daughter would have little sympathy for Malele's complaints about the village.

'Mwana, forget the town life for now. There is nothing that you can change and there is much to like here. I too, once wanted so many other things, even though I had so little schooling. I was so sure that I would not be just a village woman with children. I cried and shouted at my father to let me go to a mission to learn and to board, but there was no money and he said that girls should stay at home. I stayed and married and in the end it was for the best. I have children and grandchildren round me and all the anger is past.'

'But you are so old. I am young and times are different.'

'I said the same, mwana. Most young people do. It is hard to learn contentment, but I truly believe that it will come. Learn all you can and if God wills it, you will go back to the town and have a career there. It is what God wants and we must accept that. I also believe that one must be ready for opportunities and make the most of them. Do well at school and keep an open mind.'

'I will go back one day. I don't know how but I will.'

'Maybe, but in the meantime you are here, so learn what you can of our traditions. They are lost in the city and I believe that this should not be so.'

The old woman took Malele's hands in her own wrinkled

ones. 'See, mwana, my hands are hard and marked by life. Yours are soft and still childish. One day you will be as old as I am and what you make of your life is up to you. Don't forget that. Every day is important and will not come again. Now you think that the future is endless, but it isn't, so don't waste it in anger or wishing for something else.'

To her own surprise Malele found herself adapting to the slow tempo of the village. Gradually her resentment faded and she came to accept the way of life and to make friends.

'I am becoming a cabbage,' she told herself. 'Still, in many ways I am happy.'

There were times when she longed for the excitement of the Lusaka township, the bustle of the markets and the friends she had left behind but, as the year passed, they became like a dream and a place which she might one day go back to. She passed into Grade Nine, the top class at the school and tried not to think what she would do once the year was over. Amai brushed all her queries aside.

'Wait until the time comes, then we will see what happens.'

Her grandmother offered the same advice. 'There is a long time to go, Mwana. If I had money I would send you to a boarding school to go on with your classes, but I have none. Whatever is decided you must accept it. Remember how much you hated the village life when you came. Now you are part of it. You have friends and you understand our ways.'

'I am part of it, but not for ever, I want to have a different sort of life and to come back here just to see you all when I can. That is my dream and I want it so badly that it must happen.'

'Keep believing, mwana. Who knows what will happen.' The seasons changed and the crops were harvested. Malele helped to bring them in. News filtered through that the gang responsible for the killing of James Simonga and several other men had been arrested, and that they had been given the death

15

sentence. Jess was jubilant and said that the killers had got what they deserved and she hoped that they rotted in hell, but Malele was saddened and remembered how her father had always preached forgiveness. She was fifteen, tall and slim, with a promise of beauty to come.

One afternoon when she was doing her school work she heard Silas and her mother talking. It was unusual for Silas to visit in the afternoon and Malele was curious. She put down her book and listened.

'She is a woman now, Jess, and the schooling will end in a few months time, then we will have to decide what to do. As you know there is no money for going to boarding school, and anyway all this learning is wasted on a girl.'

'So? What do you suggest we do?'

'The girl is becoming attractive and there are men looking for suitable wives. She will fetch a good bride price and whether it is in cash or in goats it will be useful. No girl should be without a husband and she will have grandchildren for you and be settled in her life here.'

'That won't please Malele,' amai spoke sharply. 'You know how she feels about her schooling and having a career. For myself it seems the best thing for her to marry once she is sixteen. In the old days she would have been married ages ago and would have a child by now, but today that is not so.'

'Sixteen is what the Government says and not before. She will be sixteen at the end of the year and we should start looking round for a suitable husband. Only the other day Alec Zulu remarked that she would be a good wife for him now that his wife has died. He is rich and we will get a good price from him.'

'He is so old. His children are Malele's age.'

'True, but there is a shortage of young men in the village. They go off to the towns and they marry there. Alec Zulu has money and is well thought of. Age is a small thing, and an experienced husband is no bad thing for a young girl. Zulu is the best that is on the market and I will start making the necessary overtures to him. It is time we prepared for Malele's future. She has settled down here now. At first I wondered what we could do with her, but now she accepts the village life.'

'I wouldn't be too sure. Sometimes she still wants to go back to the city life.'

'It is up to you to make her obey what you tell her to do. She is not going back to the city to be a street girl which is all that will happen if we let her go. She has no real qualifications and Grade Nine is not good enough to go to a training centre even if we had the money. As far as marriage goes she did not go through the usual initiation ceremony when she became a woman, and to our village men that lessens her value. Indeed, in the past girls were killed for that.'

'I suppose you are right. As she is my daughter I have some sympathy for her ambitions, but, as you say, there is no money and no one for her to go to in Lusaka if we had money.' She sighed then went on. 'No, she will marry and that will be that.'

Malele sat stunned by what she had heard. Somehow she had always believed that she would get to boarding school and do her secondary education. Now she was to be married off, and to Alec Zulu who was old enough to be her father, and a disagreeable man who seldom had a good word for anyone.

She sat for a long time, too upset to move. Then she knew what she would do. The school year ended in December and as soon as it was over she would run away, back to Lusaka and try to find some friend who would let her stay and help her to find work. She would be almost sixteen and she would work at anything, however hard and however humble, rather than stay here and marry Alec Zulu. Malele said nothing to her mother and began to prepare for her escape.

The first thing was money. Somehow she had to get enough to get her to Lusaka and to keep her until she found work. Malele knew little about earning money and she had no real idea of how much she would need, but once the idea was in her head she started planning. She told no one, and the problem of getting money seemed to be something that she could not solve.

'I will go anyway,' she told herself defiantly. 'Even without money. I have friends in Lusaka and they will help me. There are plenty of lorries going past our village and I can get a lift on one of them.'

She wondered whether to speak to her grandmother, but Malele knew that the old woman would not approve of her running away. Several times she nearly told her the story of how she was to be married off, but something stopped her. She wondered if the old woman knew about the marriage. Nothing further had happened, but every time she saw Alec Zulu he grinned at her and made little remarks about what an attractive girl she was becoming. She hated him, his beer belly, his eyes which ranged over her body and his confident air. School would be over in three weeks and then Malele would be sixteen after the New Year and could be legally married. The grandmother said nothing when Malele told her how much she hated Alec, but there was no mention of any marriage.

'He is not a bad man,' the old woman said. 'There are worse about. Try to see the best in him. No one is perfect.'

'I know that. I just don't like him,' Malele often spoke about the man, willing her grandmother to say something to show that she knew what was planned, but nothing was said.

'I am getting old, Malele,' she said one day as they sat together. 'I have a little money saved ... only very little ... but it is buried under my bed mat. I mean it for you to use one day.'

Malele listened and wondered. Was this a sign for her to

18

take the money? Did the old woman know and disapprove of the marriage plans? She dared not ask, so nodded her thanks. Esnart's face was expressionless but her eyes twinkled.

'You will live for a long time more,' Malele said. 'So don't talk about when you are gone.'

'Perhaps. Who knows. Life is a funny thing. One is here, then one is gone and the body is in the ground. Still, this is morbid talk and meaningless. I just wanted you to know about the money.'

Chapter 3

The school closed and Malele sadly said goodbye to her teacher.

'It is a pity that you aren't going on to senior school,' he said. 'You are bright enough, but that's how things are. Your mother said that there was no money for it.'

'No money,' Malele repeated. 'I so wanted to go on. And now I will just be at home and no career at all.'

'That's how things are,' he repeated. 'Perhaps one day your children will have the opportunities that you do not. One day there will be education for all.'

Malele shook her head.

'Maybe, but I need it now and not later. If only things were different. If only my father hadn't died and if only I had stayed at the school in Lusaka. There are so many if onlys.'

'In all our lives there are things that we wished had happened, but you are young and have all your life in front of you to enjoy.'

'I am young, but I wonder how much of my life I will enjoy?' Malele spoke quietly.

Suddenly she was afraid of what she was about to do, and the unknown things that would happen to her when she ran away. She forced the thoughts away.

'One makes what one can of life,' the teacher said. 'Be prepared for anything and enjoy what you can. If you can't change something make the best of it.'

'I will.' Malele left him and her school days ended. She would have a few weeks to get ready, then she must leave.

Amai brought up the subject of marriage, not meeting her eyes as she spoke. 'Well, Malele, you have done well at school and have passed grade nine. There is no more that the school here can teach you so it is time that we thought about your future.'

20

Malele waited, a wild hope surging through her that her mother would say that she was to go on to a boarding school.

'You will be sixteen very soon, and it is time that you settled down. The village life is a good one and this is where you belong.' Malele's hopes dropped like a stone.

'The good news is that there is someone who wants to have you as his wife and he is an important man.' Malele stared at her mother and said nothing. Let amai tell her what she already knew. She would not make it easy for amai.

'Don't you want to know who he is? I thought that you would be excited by the news. 'Still Malele said nothing.

'The man is Alec Zulu and he has asked Silas if he can marry you when you are sixteen.'

'Alec Zulu?' Malele spat the words out. 'Amai, do you really think that I want to be his wife? He is old and dreadful apart from anything else, and why should I become a second wife? His children are older than I am. I heard you and Silas talking long ago and I said nothing because I hoped that you would love me enough to change your mind, but you haven't. I heard you say that the bride price would be good and you want to sell me like some sort of animal just because you want to be rid of me.'

The tears were running down her cheeks and anger was making her voice harsh. 'Let me tell you, amai, I will not marry that old man. I hate him and the way he looks at me, undressing me with his eyes. There is no way that I will have him, whatever you do or say.'

'You have no choice. We are dependent on Silas who is your father's brother and he is the one who has agreed to the marriage. You should be grateful that someone with many cattle and goats wants you, and age has nothing to do with it. He only seems old because you are so young. Now, stop crying, my child, and try to accept what we have planned for you. Remember how you cried when you came to the village?

21

Now it is part of your life. Things change, especially when one is young.

'I won't change. The village has been my home, but I have always wanted to leave and go on to school. You know that. I never wanted to stay for ever, and certainly not to marry here. I want a career, not to be some man's slave.'

'You are talking nonsense. What career can you have? Grade Nine is fine, but not enough to have a career and you have finished school for ever. Being a wife is a good thing, and when the children come you will be too busy and too happy to think of a career.'

'That's what you think. Amai, you have always been a village woman, even when you went to the town. That is how you are but I am different. I will not marry that old man.'

'You have no choice.' Jess's brows drew together in anger, and her lips were set in a hard straight line. 'Now, no more nonsense. You will not be sixteen for a while, so you will get used to the idea. Think of all the advantages of being married to such an important man.'

Malele fled to her grandmother and sobbed out her story. 'I knew about it before, ambuya, and I said nothing, for I kept believing that amai would somehow change and would be able to let me go to school. I couldn't believe that in the end she would sell me like some goat.'

'Hush, mwana. I, too, hoped that she would change for your sake, but Zulu is well off and not such a bad catch. A bit old perhaps, but age is not necessarily a problem. What else could you do? There is no money for the boarding school and Silas thinks that the education that you have had already is wasted on a girl. Men will change one day, but not now. You are too young to go to the city and without any skills or experience in the way of work. You would starve there, or end by selling your body to men for money in order to survive. That has happened to so many girls. Men are predators on the young women who need money.'

'I know all that. I know about AIDS and about sex. Remember I came from the city where we were taught about such things. Grandmother Esnart, I will not marry Zulu, whatever they say. I will run away and never come back. Anything rather than marrying him.'

'To run away would be foolish. You are too young and too unskilled and would only end up worse off than now. Mwana, accept things that you cannot change and maybe one day you will find some way for a career after marriage. These things can happen.'

'I will not be sold like an animal.'

'Until you are eighteen you must obey your family. That is the law and cannot be changed. I wish that things could be different, but remember that they could be so much worse. Here, we love you and are your family. You have friends too. They will marry like you and their children will be friends of your children. It is not so bad.'

'How can you say that, ambuya? Even you want me married off and kept here. I thought that you would be on my side. Now I know that no one cares and I am alone,' Malele sobbed harder. 'Even you want me married off.'

'It is not my choice, but I accept what Silas and my daughter decide. Malele, you must grow up and make the best of this. When I am dead there will be the very small bit of money that I have under the bed mat and perhaps it will buy you some small thing to remember me by. Apart from that all I can offer is an old woman's advice ... marry and enjoy your family. Put your impractical ideas aside until one day they may be practical.'

Esnart hugged the girl, her old hands smoothing her hair as she comforted her. Malele could smell the wood smoke on her and feel the frail bones of her body.

There was tension between Malele and her family as the days went by. Alec Zulu took to visiting and tried to make conversation with Malele who ignored him.

'You are a rude, ungrateful girl,' Jess scolded. 'The least you can do is to try to be pleasant. You are sour and difficult and if you are not careful he will become angry with you and decide that you will need a strong hand once he marries you.'

Malele began her plans for escape. Money was the problem. Without it she could not go. She could probably get a lift with a truck so the journey was not the problem. The real problem would be keeping herself until she found a friend or work in Lusaka.

'Hidden under my bed mat.' The words kept coming back to her. Ambuya must have been telling her for a reason, and the reason could only have been to let her know that it was available if she needed it. The old woman would not openly go against Jess and Silas, but if Malele just slipped into the hut and took the money she could honestly say that she knew nothing.

Late one afternoon, while her grandmother was collecting water from the stream, Malele slipped into the hut. Her heart was beating fast and she was afraid of being seen, but once she was inside and her eyes adjusted to the darkness, Malele moved the bed mat away and scrabbled in the earth where she could see it had been disturbed not so long ago. The money was in a small tin and Malele lifted it out, then carefully replaced the earth, smoothing it and replacing the mat. She had thought of putting a note into the cavity, saying that she had taken the money, but ambuya could not read, so Malele put a string of beads there instead. Ambuya would recognise them and understand.

Everything was very quiet as she cautiously pushed aside the reed mat over the door and went out into the evening light. Down the path she could see ambuya walking slowly, weighed down by the pot of water that she carried. Malele pushed the tin into her chitenge and hurried off, before ambuya came close. The old woman's sight was bad so she would not notice a figure in the distance.

Once in her own hut Malele counted the money. It was all in small denomination notes and coins and must have represented a long time of saving. In all there was twelve thousand kwacha. To Malele it was enough for her escape. The money would soon be used up, but she was confident that she would find one of her friends in Lusaka and be allowed to stay with their family until she could find some work. Her plans were imprecise and her knowledge of conditions in Lusaka were based on her childish days there, two years ago, but Malele brushed all her doubts and fears aside. She was going and that was that. She would somehow manage. She sorted out her few clothes; two chitenge cloths and two T-shirts and little else. They made a small bundle which she tied in a headscarf.

That evening at supper she was very silent, thinking about her great adventure. Alec Zulu had been round to visit the family and his presence made her even more determined to go. She would leave a note for amai, just to say that she had decided to go, but apart from that there would be no goodbyes. Her friends would wonder where she was and then forget her.

Very early in the morning she picked up her bundle, made sure that the money was knotted in her chitenge cloth and crept out of her hut. The stars were fading in the sky and a dog barked as she passed, but there was no one about and the path to the roadside was deserted. The trucks would come with the sun, grinding along the steep road on their way to Lusaka.

Malele reached the road and waited. She was worried that she might have been missed and that amai would come looking for her once she had read the note. It seemed a long time before there was any sound of traffic and Malele became increasingly anxious. The sun was bright and people would soon be coming along the road and along the village path. Far off she could hear a truck, its engine sound deepening as the driver changed gears on the gradient and she heaved a sigh of relief. It was a battered Leyland truck, loaded with grain bags.

She stepped into the road and waved. The lorry stopped and the driver peered out of the cab.

'Please can you take me to Lusaka? Are you going there? I need to get there to see a sick relative.' The lie came easily.

'You are in luck. This load is to go to Lusaka and no stopping on the way.'

Malele clambered into the cab beside the lorry boy and the driver. The driver was an elderly man. He looked closely at Malele before he started off.

'You are young to be alone asking for lifts on the main road. If you were my daughter I would not like it.'

'I am seventeen although I look younger. I am not a child.' She wished that he would start off before any one came and saw her, but having got into the cab she had no intention of losing the lift. 'My mother is ill in Lusaka and needs me,' she explained. 'My father is away and there is no one at home but my grandmother so I have to travel alone. I would have taken the bus but we have no money.'

'I won't harm you, mwana, but there are many men who would. It is not safe to take lifts along the road. Young women are not able to take care of themselves … The official bus is best, but I suppose that money is the problem.'

'It is a problem, but if I get to Lusaka I have relatives there so there will be no problem.' She smiled at him again. He had accepted her story, but she felt a bit mean at having to lie to him.

The driver revved up the engine and much to Malele's relief they started off again. She looked back, but there was no sign of anyone coming from the village. She settled down against the seat and watched the trees and grass pass by. The noise of the engine made conversation difficult and she was content not to talk. She had told enough lies already and would have to remember what she had said. That was the trouble with lies. One was so often caught out.

The journey took eight hours with a short break for a Fanta and something to eat. Malele was offered part of the lunch that the driver had with him and, with hunger gnawing at her, she was pleased to accept.

'Your grandmother should have given you food for the journey,' the driver said as they ate. 'It is a long journey with no food to eat.'

'She meant to,' lied Malele, 'but I left very early in case I missed a lift.' She was tired and aching from the swaying of the truck when they reached Lusaka.

'Where do you meet your relatives?' the old man asked.

'If it is near where I am going I will drop you there. It will be getting dark before too long and Lusaka is no place for a young girl to wander about at night.'

Malele thought quickly. She remembered that the bus station was the place where people slept while waiting for transport, and as there was no one to meet her it seemed the easiest place to go. She would sleep there for the night and then try to find some friend to stay with.

'The bus station. That is where I will be met.'

'Right. That is where I will drop you off. Now, mwana, wait there for your friend. Don't try to go out and find her. The bus station is always full of people and you should be safe there until you are collected.' His concern sounded in his voice. Malele reassured him. 'I will wait, but I expect that my friend will be waiting for me, so don't worry. You have been so kind in bringing me here.'

The bus station was busy with the big long distance vehicles coming and going, passengers disembarking and passengers pushing for seats. Malele thanked the driver and watched him drive off. For a moment she felt afraid and alone, then, pulling herself together, she clutched her bundle firmly under her arm, checked that the money was safely tied in her chitenge cloth and walked into the hall. She had arrived at last

27

and the village and her mother were far away. The big adventure was about to begin.

Back in the village, Jess wept angry tears when she found that Malele had run away. She was concerned about the safety of the girl but it was the loss of face and the scandal that would inevitably ensue that worried her the most. Alec Zulu was an important man in the district and would be furious with the whole family. Silas was angry too.

'Have you no control over your daughter?' He demanded as Jess sobbed out her story.

'I have promised her to Alec Zulu, and I have even had the bride price for her. Now I will have to sell the cattle that I have bought with the money and pay him back. Of all ungrateful girls! I have given her a home and fed her all this time and this is how she repays me. Are you sure that she has gone?' He had a faint hope that she was only hiding nearby.

'She has gone. Someone saw her getting onto a lorry. Lusaka is a big place and she may go there.'

'Or she may stop off somewhere along the way. I blame you for this Jess. She is your daughter and you should have watched her better. Now I will have to tell Zulu what has happened and it is all your fault. There is no way we can get her back I suppose?'

Alec Zulu was furious. It was not so much the loss of Malele that angered him as the disgrace of having his chosen bride run away rather than marry him.

'I will be the laughing stock of the village,' he roared.

'She is a foolish girl and has brought disgrace to your family. Get her back at once and I will still have her, but otherwise I will say that I have decided not to marry her and she has run away because of that. And I want my money back.'

Malele had gone and there was no way of forcing her to return, so Zulu let it be known that it was he who had chased her away, and Silas had to repay the bride price.

'No one really believes him,' Esnart said quietly.

'However, it saves face and that is a good thing. I just hope that Malele is all right in the big city.' She did not tell Jess that it was her money that had provided the escape.

Chapter 4

Malele pushed her way into the ladies toilet. The acrid smell of the lavatories made her gasp and she found that the water in the basin taps was a mere trickle, hardly enough to wash her face and hands. Women were feeding their babies, changing their clothes and there was a constant chattering and noise. The girl dried her hands and face on her chitenge as there were no towels. She was hungry and had taken a few notes out from her hoard of money while she was in the toilet and no one could see her. She would have to find something to eat and then some corner to sleep in. As she went out of the rest-room door, the money clutched in one hand, the bundle in the other, a man bumped into her, half-knocking her over. She almost dropped the precious clothes and by the time she had recovered her balance, the man had disappeared into the crowd and she realised that he had taken the money which was in her hand. Malele gave a small cry and stood helplessly looking at her empty palm. It had happened so quickly and now she had lost the food money. In a panic she felt in her chitenge and with a great relief her fingers found the knot of money still safe.

'I saw it, mwana, 'a woman said, coming up to the girl. 'I saw that thief take the money from your hand. It happens so often. The thief sees you with something that he wants and so he almost knocks you over and snatches the prize. Mwana, be warned. It so often happens. Are you from out of town? Is there no one with you?'

'No. I am alone, but someone will come for me.' Malele was shocked and upset. 'He took all the money that I had for food.' She felt hot tears behind her eyes and blinked angrily to stop them from spilling over. 'It was a horrible thing to do.'

'It happens. A girl alone is an easy victim. Never carry money in your hand for people to see. It is asking for trouble.'

'I have found that out.' Malele's voice was choked. 'It was so sudden and I did not even feel him take the money. I was too busy saving my balance.'

'Well, be careful. I have a bus to catch and must go.'

The stout woman went off leaving Malele. Back in the lavatory the girl took a few precious notes from her chitenge. The roll of notes seemed pathetically small. Back in the village it had represented freedom, but now it was all that she had to keep herself. In the cracked mirror she stared at herself, her eyes wide and frightened, then she lifted her chin and tossed her head defiantly.

'I am glad that I came. I am going to make a good life for myself.' The words had a hollow ring but they made her feel better and she forced herself to believe them. One of the women near her looked surprised, but Malele smiled at her and ignored her.

She was cautious when she pushed open the door of the ladies restroom and entered the bustling hallway. The money was clenched tightly in her fist. She pushed through the crowd to a small stall which sold buns and other food plus soft drinks and cups of tea. The bun was stale and the tea weak and tepid but Malele was so hungry that she hardly noticed and when she had finished, she wished that she could afford more. She was walking across the hall when she saw the man who had taken her money. He was standing laughing with a friend, his hands in his pockets and lolling against a bench. Impulsively Malele went towards him, anger making her determined to speak to him. He glanced down at her as she came up to him.

'You took my money when I came out of the restroom,' Malele said accusingly. 'I want it back. I have little enough without sharing it with you.' She held out her hand.

'Mwana, what are you talking about?' He grinned at her. 'What money?'

'You know what money. You are a thief and I want my money back.'

He laughed. 'You are mad, mwana. All this talk about money. If you want money come with me and we will see what happens outside. It depends how accommodating you are.'

'You know what I mean,' Malele shouted, her temper overcoming common-sense. People were stopping to watch the scene.

The man turned to his friend. 'This mwana has a loud voice and she says bad things.'

'Call a policeman,' his friend advised. 'You need protection from this prostitute. Here we are minding our own business and she comes along shouting.'

Malele stamped her foot. 'I am not a prostitute and I want the money he stole from me. I have a witness who saw you take it.'

As she said it, Malele realised that the woman had probably left on one of the buses that were constantly leaving the depot and she had no way of finding her.

The man turned away, taunting her with his knowing grin.

'Hey, mwana. I am a patient man, but this is getting serious. If I call the policeman he will lock you up for the night. Either go and shut up or I will do just that.'

Malele was frightened. The police would do nothing to help her even if they could, and there was no way she could prove that he had stolen the money.

'I hope that the money does you harm,' she said angrily.

'No good will come of stealing.'

She walked off, ignoring the spectators and their comments, and hearing the men laughing behind her. Her hands were shaking. She would have to spend the night here and then she could walk to the township where she had lived. Her best friend, Shamba, would be there and perhaps Malele could stay with her for a short while. She remembered how Shamba and she had talked during their days at school, making plans for when they left school and took up a career. When Malele left, Shamba had said that one day Malele would be back and all the good things would happen as planned. That was two years ago and Malele hoped that things would still be the same. Two years was a long time but they had been close friends and Shamba's mother had been a friend of Jess too. That might be a problem. Parents were apt to stick together over daughters running away. Malele refused to think about it.

The night was long and cold and Malele slept fitfully, sitting on a hard metal bench, her bundle on her knees in case someone tried to take it. All through the night people came and went. Even in the small hours of the morning there were people moving about and there was some noise.

Early in the morning, Malele left the bus station and started on the long walk to the township. The route was achingly familiar and made her remember all sorts of things that had happened during her stay in Lusaka. Her father had been here with her, her mother had taken her to the market there, she had played with Shamba in that park.

'I hate the way the past creeps in,' Malele said aloud. 'It is what is happening now that matters. The past has gone and I have no time for it now. Maybe when I am old, but not now.'

When she reached the township she kept looking out for anyone that she knew, but the people that she passed were unfamiliar. As it was so early many of them were on their way to work and were hurrying to catch buses or to meet deadlines. There were school children dressed in their uniforms walking to their classes at the first session of school. Later they would be free to come home and another group would take their places in the classrooms. Most schools operated in the three session system. Malele wondered what Shamba would be doing, the senior schools had only two, so Shamba might still be at home.

Her old house looked much the same as when she had lived there, but someone had cut down the avocado pear tree which grew by the tap. A woman was standing in the doorway as Malele passed. Shamba's home was nearby and Malele

33

quickened her step. She had no plans as to what she would say and if Shamba's family refused to have her, she had decided that she would have to go back to the bus stop and stay there until she could find work and some sort of accommodation.

'Shamba,' Malele shouted as she approached the house. Her friend had come out of the doorway, dressed in her uniform, satchel on her back, ready to go to school. Shamba looked startled, then recognised Malele.

'Malele, whatever are you doing here? I thought I was seeing a ghost or something.'

Malele laughed as she hugged Shamba. 'No ghost. I have run away from the village because they wanted to marry me off to an awful old man. I couldn't go to boarding school as there is no money.'

'It sounds dreadful. What are you going to do here?'

'Try to find some sort of work ... anything at all so that I can support myself. I have so little money and I need a place to stay.'

'To stay?' Shamba seemed to distance herself from Malele. 'Where are you living now?'

'At the bus station. I only came last night and now I am trying to find somewhere, at least until I find work.'

'I wish that we could have you, but we have cousins staying with us and my mother keeps complaining about too many people in the house.'

Malele could sense her friend's embarrassment and pride made her say, 'Oh, I am not asking you for help. I am managing all right. I just came to see you.'

'That was nice of you. Things are hard here and I don't know how much longer I will be able to stay at school. Now I must hurry off. It has been lovely seeing you again, Malele. Good luck with your job hunting and I will be seeing you sometime.' Her words dismissed Malele. She was obviously unwilling to do more.

Shamba hurried off leaving Malele feeling abandoned.

Her one-time friend had changed so much. All the old intimacy had evaporated in the past two years and Shamba obviously had her own life and its attendant problems. Malele was stunned by the change, but of course it had been unrealistic to expect Shamba and her family to help. There was no one else that she felt she could turn to. All her father's relatives lived in other parts of the country now and her other friends had really been not much more than casual acquaintances.

'I would have tried to persuade my mother to help,' Malele thought. 'I wouldn't have changed like that.'

Thinking about it as she walked back to the town Malele had to admit that she too had changed. Two years was a long time at her stage of life and both of them had changed. Full of disappointment, she trudged along the verge of the dusty road, the stones and the dust making her feet sore. The bundle was heavy and the sun was getting hot.

When she reached Cairo Road where many of the big shops were, Malele walked along the potholed pavements, envying the people who were working in the shops and keeping a sharp lookout for any notices that offered jobs. There were several, but the posts wanted more than a grade nine certificate and in any case Malele had not received hers before she left the village. Depression hung heavily over her as she walked; she had been so sure that she would find some sort of job easily once she had reached Lusaka. In the same way she had been sure that Shamba would somehow let her stay. To cheer herself up she hummed a tune that she had learned as a child. A young man made a crude comment as she passed, whistling admiringly, but Malele gave him a discouraging stare and walked on.

The market place was full of people, the makeshift stalls displaying all kinds of goods ranging from fruit and vegetables to secondhand clothing, salaula, which came in bales from the United States as support for the third world poor. She examined some of the dresses, pretending that she was interested in buying and imagining herself in them. One or two stallholders asked if they could help in making the choice, but Malele shook her head and went on to the other stalls. She knew that she was wasting time and that she should be doing something more constructive like finding a job, but the disappointment of Shamba combined with hunger made her lethargic. One woman behind a fruit stall looked kindly and Malele asked her if she knew of any work for her to do.

'There is no work now. Everyone is short of money and there are so few jobs going that one need all sorts of education to even apply. Where have you come from that you don't know that? The village has more to offer these days. What can you do, mwana. You look young and what experience do you have? Are you a housemaid or a secretary?'

'No, but I am a grade nine and I can write well and I am willing to work hard. I need a job.'

'There are hundreds of grade nines looking for work. Have you a national registration card? Employers want that first, even before they think about you.'

Malele had forgotten about the registration card. It was obtainable from the Labour Office when one was sixteen, but it took time and money to get one, and she was not quite sixteen.

'I have lost mine,' she said. 'I am waiting for a new one.'

'Well, get it first then maybe something will turn up. Sometimes in the market there are jobs for people without cards, but they are badly paid and it is illegal to take on such people. A few of the expatriates take on maids but they want experienced women, and the local rich rely on their extended family for cheap labour most of the time. Have you no family?'

'I have, but they have gone back to the village and I want to stay here.'

'You would do better to go with them. You are very young to be alone and I can offer no help.'

Malele sighed. 'You have helped by talking to me.'

She wanted to tell this sympathetic stranger her story, but caution held her back. Perhaps Jess would report her missing and some policeman might make a few enquiries. The woman picked up an orange and handed it to the girl.

'Here. This will sweeten things for you. I am sorry that it is all I can offer you.'

The unexpected kindness choked Malele. She wished that she could stay near this stranger and not have to go back to the bus station but, having thanked her, she left the stall and in the evening, when the marketeers were packing up for the night, Malele walked back to the station.

Nshima and relish was being sold by an elderly woman who had set up her wares outside the station. The smell of the food made Malele realise how little she had eaten over the past twenty-four hours.

'I have to have food,' she told herself. 'One meal a day is enough, but I have to have that however much I want to save money.'

The foodseller was alone when Malele approached her, the few notes clutched securely in her hand. The coals reflected in the puddles that had formed during an earlier shower and the smoke spiralled up from the brazier. It was chilly and Malele held out her hands to the warmth.

'Eh, the rain has made things cold,' said the woman, her smile was gap-toothed. 'Do you want some nshima and relish. It is cheap here and I do not cheat my customers.'

She lifted some of the steaming mealie meal out of the pot and placed it in a plastic plate. 'You look hungry so I will put a bit extra in. Business is bad tonight. The rain always does that, but people will come again soon, now that the rain is over. I charge only five pin for the mealie meal and the relish.'

Malele held out the five thousand kwacha note, reluctant to pay out her precious money, but her stomach was rumbling and her mouth watering at the sight of the food.

'Thank you, ambuya. I am hungry and this has made me want food even more.' She took the plate and the woman ladled a piece of meat and some vegetables with gravy onto another plate and held it out to her.

'Eat, mwana, and stay near the warmth and talk to me. What are you doing here alone? I saw you arrive last night when a lorry stopped and you got out. Why are you still here and not at home?'

The food was filling Malele's thoughts. She rolled a piece of the stiff porridge between her fingers in the time-honoured way and dipped it in the relish, then filled her mouth with the savoury food.

'I am looking for work, ambuya. That is why I am here.' There seemed no point in not telling the woman and the warmth and the food made her want to have company. She sat down on a brick, her bundle between her feet.

'This is no place to search for work. You are very young. How old are you?'

'Seventeen, but I have lost my registration card and now it is hard to get work. I have passed grade nine, but my father has died and there is no money for me to go on at school. I need a job and I am a hard worker.'

'What can you do? Have you any experience?'

'No, very little, but I know how to sweep and clean and I can read and write. Don't you know of anything that I can do? I thought that it would be easy to find work, but now I know that it is a problem.'

'No registration card is a problem to add to all the others, and it costs to get a new one as well as taking a long time.'

There was silence for a while as Malele ate and the woman served another customer. Malele wiped the last of the mealie meal over the relish plate, then handed the plates back to the woman. 'Thank you, ambuya. That food was so good. My mother cooks like you do and everyone says that she is a good cook.' She smiled and wished that she could afford more.

She was still hungry.

'Where do you come from?'

'A village near Chipata, ambuya. I want to work in the town and not stay there. That is why I have come.'

'And your mother let you, without having a relative to go to? What sort of a mother is that? Did you just run away like so many?'

Malele hung her head. The foodseller was looking hard at her as though she knew exactly what the truth was. 'They wanted to marry me to an old man,' Malele said slowly. 'It would have been worse than coming here and finding no work. My grandmother, Esnart Banda, had a little money so I have that, but I have very little.'

'A sorry tale, mwana. Young girls are so keen to live in town. I can sympathize. I, too, would not wish to live in the village as I did once when I was young. Still, it is a silly thing to do without proper thought. In the end so many sell their bodies to men for money and get HIV. They have no other way of living and it ends in them dying.' She paused and stayed silent for a while.

'I knew an Esnart Banda once. She lived in Katemo village and when we were young women we were friends. She was married and she always wanted to see the city but then the children came and I married and left. I have never gone back. I had not thought of her for many years.'

'My grandmother still lives in that village. Oh, ambuya. Perhaps my grandmother was your friend all those years ago. It could be the same person. My grandmother is old now, but when she was young she wanted to do great things.'

'Perhaps we once knew each other, but that was long ago. There are other Esnart Bandas.'

'My grandmother has a scar on her arm where she was burnt when her house caught fire... her right arm above her wrist.'

'Eh, and so had my friend. I can remember the night it

happened and all the excitement and all the loss. It must indeed be my friend. Eh, how strange that you should come to me like that. What is your name?'

'Malele. My mother is Jess, her firstborn.'

'Jess ... yes, she was born before I married and went to Lusaka. Esnart was older than me and if I thought of her at all, I must have thought her dead.'

'She seems very old now.'

'So do I to you. Youth always thinks their seniors older than they are. Malele. Malele.' She repeated the name a few times reflectively.

'Who would have thought it. After all these years. Did you tell Esnart that you were leaving?'

'No, but I think she knew, and I left her a note ... and one to my mother so they will not worry.'

'Maybe not, but because of our old friendship I now feel that I must at least try to help you. I live with my son as my husband is dead. He was born late in my life and he is all I have. He works and I earn by selling food. Is that all you have with you?'

'Only this bundle, ambuya. Oh ambuya, to think that you were my grandmother's friend. Please help me to find a job, and then I will earn money and make a life for myself.'

Chapter 5

Malele followed the foodseller home that night, her bundle in one hand and the heavy porridge pot in the other. She was to stay with the woman and her son until she found somewhere to go. The thought of having a proper place to sleep and somewhere as a base, filled Malele with hope. After all, it had been almost a miracle finding her grandmother's old friend and she had spent a lot of time answering questions about the people who had lived in the village when Eunice Phiri had been there.

'Ambuya, I have only lived there for two years and most of those people are no longer there. Perhaps they have moved or perhaps they are dead. My grandmother would know, or even my mother.'

'I would write to your grandmother if I could write better, but one day perhaps we will meet if God is willing. You must write to her for me and tell her that you are safe. It was not right to go off like that even if you didn't like the man. Modern girls have no respect for customs which have been with us for many lifetimes.'

'I will have a career, ambuya, then you will be proud of me and agree that I was right. Wait and see.'

'You nearly had no career except on the streets, mwana, and don't you forget it. It was so lucky that we met.'

'I know, and I believe that I will be lucky. I don't know how, but it will come.'

Eunice Phiri grumbled on about the youth of today, but Malele was deep in her own dreams and after her depression of the day, she was full of hope for the future. Something would turn up and somehow she would achieve success. The streets were unlit as they entered the township and Malele stumbled along the unfamiliar route. She was tired and the pot and the bundle made her arms ache.

'Here we are.' Eunice turned into a narrow muddy path and there was a light shining inside the small building.

'This is my home. My son will be awake. You will share my room for there are only three rooms altogether. Boniface will be surprised to see you, but he is a good son and will not go against what I say.'

She pushed the wooden door open and the lantern light seemed bright after the darkness outside. The man who came forward to greet them was supporting himself on two crutches and Malele could see that his legs were encased in steel callipers. The sight of him shocked her. She had not expected to find the son like this and she carefully avoided looking at his legs. To her, he was a poor twisted cripple, but as she glanced at Eunice, she could see all the pride and love for her son in her face.

'Boniface, I have brought this girl home to stay with us. She was at the bus stop and has nowhere to go. While we were talking I found that she is the daughter of an old friend from the village. This is Malele and here is my son, Boniface.'

'Muli bwanji, Boniface,' Malele said.

The man nodded a greeting, his white teeth gleaming in the lamplight. There were deep pain lines between his brows and his cheeks were hollowed. He appeared indifferent to her and started speaking to his mother. Malele wondered where he worked as he would find it hard to do anything very physically active. She was afraid that he was annoyed at her being there and was uncomfortable at being ignored.

The next morning he was gone early, after a small meal of yesterday's nshima. Malele watched his crooked progress down the road to the bus stop and saw him swing himself onto the bus. They had hardly had time to do more than exchange greetings that morning and Malele had been thankful to go to bed soon after they arrived, leaving mother and son to talk. The girl had fallen asleep almost at once and had dreamed of the village and a young grandmother escaping from a burning hut.

'Where does he work?' Malele asked Eunice as the two of them cleaned the house and prepared the relish for another day's selling.

'He works the telephones for a business company in Rhodes Park. The bus passes close by and the company is a good and caring one so they don't mind about his difficulties.'

'What happened?'

'They say he had polio. When he was a small child he was so agile and so active, then he became ill and when the illness passed, his legs no longer worked properly and he became as you see him now.'

'How terrible for him. He must have hated it.'

'He did. At first he cried and wanted to join his friends, but that was impossible. My husband began to blame me for Boniface's illness and then he left me for someone else. That was a bad time and when my husband disappeared I had to support my son. I am a good cook so I started selling food and so far I have managed. Boniface went to school up to Grade Twelve, then he wanted to leave and to work. God was looking after us and he found a job where he could be seated and his legs didn't matter. He has been there for five years now.'

'He must have so much courage, ambuya.'

'I am proud of him and I thank God for him every day. I have asked him to try to find a vacant job that you could do. He has friends in the places round the office and sometimes he hears of someone leaving and a job is there. In the meantime you can help me and for that I will feed you and you can stay here. At least for a time.'

'Thank you. But are you sure that your son doesn't mind my being here?'

'He said little last night, but he is like that. Sometimes I know that he has pain, and he is shy with strangers. He will get to know you and then you will see how kind he is.'

Malele refused to think what would happen if she did not find work. Let each day look after itself. She would manage, something would happen for the better. Selling the nshima and relish occupied her for most of the day and late into the night. When it rained there were few customers and she and Eunice huddled under cover until it stopped, protecting the brazier from the damp. Then they moved to a better position near the bus station entrance where more people came and went.

'I have regular customers,' Eunice explained. 'They know that I cook well and that the food is always good. That is the only way to do things. When I first started it was hard because no one knew me, but now I have friends who buy regularly.'

Malele found the customers fascinating. There were workers from the construction company who were building across the road, workers from the bus station, travellers and a number of office and shop workers. Eunice knew most of them and Malele found that they soon greeted her. She began to feel part of the scene, but there was always the nagging knowledge that this was only temporary and that she must find some permanent post. Boniface had been unsuccessful in his enquiries for work for her. There was nothing in his area, but he was keeping a lookout.

Malele seldom saw much of the man. He left early and she returned late, but one Sunday as she waited for Eunice to finish cooking the relish, Malele found herself alone with Boniface. He was carrying some books and as she watched they slipped out of his hands. Quickly she bent to pick them up and saw that they were text- books on accountancy.

'These look very difficult books,' she remarked as she handed them back to him. 'Are you studying accounts?'
He nodded. 'I am taking a correspondence course and doing the work in the evenings when my mother is out.'

Malele was impressed. 'Will you be an accountant one day?'

'If I work and finish the course. As you can see there are limits to what I can do, but my brain is all right even if my legs are not.' He said it bitterly and the girl realized how much his handicap had blighted his life.

'Brains are the most important. Not so many people have them and if you are an accountant you will be able to get a good job.'

'I hope so. My mother is getting old and I want to be able to keep her well.' It was the first time that they had talked for any length of time and after that he began to greet her and to exchange comments with her. He told her about his school days and how he had felt awkward at being so lame, and how he was teased at first, but gradually the other children accepted him and acknowledged that he was the cleverest in the class.

'But I would have given my brain to be good at athletics,' he said wryly. 'Those good at sport were always the most sought after, not the studious ones. Not that I had any choice as when the others were on the sports fields, I was alone and had nothing better to do than study.'

'It has paid off,' Malele said. 'The athletes grow old but the clever ones go on to greater things.'

'Maybe.'

He was waiting for her one night when she returned with Eunice. 'Good news, Malele, or perhaps it is. There is a vacancy for a cleaner at the art gallery near my office. The woman that they had has gone to get married in Kitwe so they are looking for someone. If you come to work with me tomorrow I will introduce you to my friend and he will see what he can do to fix you up. He is a gallery attendant so he knows the boss.'

Malele was full of happiness. This might be the break that she wanted and she thanked Boniface effusively. 'That is wonderful, Boniface. Thank you. Of course I will go with you in the morning.'

'I can't promise that they will take you,' Boniface

cautioned her. 'However it is a possibility.'

Eunice beamed. 'Let's hope they will. Now Malele, have you money for the bus fare. One pin.'

'Yes. Won't it be wonderful if I get the job, ambuya? Then I will be earning.'

'Wait and see and don't build your hopes on it.'

The next morning Malele and Boniface took the bus to Rhodes Park and he introduced her to his friend at the art gallery.

'I have told the boss that I would be bringing someone,' Petson Ndjovu said. 'Come on. He gets in about nine hours most days and if we hurry I can show you round the place.'

Malele followed the tall young man across the road and into the back entrance of the gallery. It was an old colonial house which had been converted into a gallery. The kitchen was much as it had been, but the wood stove had been taken out and a small microwave put on one of the counters. Malele didn't know what the microwave was and Petson laughed.

'Hey, Malele. You really are from the sticks. I thought that everyone knew about these things. Get with it, man. This is the new age cooking. To hell with the old wood stove.'

Malele felt his scorn. 'Sorry, but in the village we don't have microwaves, and nor did we when I lived in town. I'll catch up so don't worry.' She was annoyed with his superior air. 'I bet you don't have a microwave at your home so stop trying to show off.'

'Girl has a sharp tongue,' he joked. 'I like women with spirit even if they do come from the sticks and don't know anything. Come on, never mind modern science, I will show you the gallery and you can see what some of the artists call art.'

The gallery extended to three rooms, well-lit with spotlights beamed onto the paintings and the sculptures. Some of the paintings pleased Malele as she could understand what they represented, but others were a mass of lines and colour and she could make no sense of them.

'Ha! Bet that means nothing to you, girl from the sticks.' Petson indicated a large canvass full of colour.

'That is called "Joyful Day" and the artist wants one thousand dollars for it.'

'A thousand dollars?' Malele knew that this was a great deal of money. 'I can't understand it at all and if I had a thousand dollars I would not waste it on this.'

'This is modern art and one day you may get to understand it. The artists tell me that it expresses their souls, so who am I to argue. People do pay for the work and so the rest of us here get our salaries.'

'I see.' She inspected a carved wooden form inlaid with brass strips. 'And this?'

'It is called Standing Form and is by a man called Castro. He sells plenty and people like his work.'

'So do I in a way, even though I have no idea what it is.' She touched the smooth curved surface with her fingertips. 'I do like it.'

'I am sure that the artist will value your opinion.' Petson grinned. 'A girl from the sticks likes what he does.'

'Can't you shut up about my being from the sticks? I have passed grade nine and I am not so ignorant.'

Malele thought of all sorts of scathing things to say to him, but as he was trying to get her a job she held her tongue and wandered round the rest of the gallery. They passed through a doorway into a courtyard where there were two men working on paintings and another carving a figure.

'These are some of the gallery artists. The boss lets them work here and the public come to watch sometimes. All part of the business.' No one paid any attention to Malele.

'Come on, the boss will be here soon and I will take you to him.'

Malele waited in the kitchen, anxiously dusting her shoes and wishing that she had something smart to wear, even though the position was only that of a cleaner. Her simple chitenge and T-shirt seemed out of place and she felt the truth of Petson's description of a girl from the sticks. She had glimpsed a very smart-looking girl with long hair extensions and a stylish dress sitting in the office. That was how she wanted to be.

'One day, one day,' she muttered to herself.

The smart young woman appeared in the doorway, her impersonal gaze resting on Malele with barely concealed contempt. 'You have come for the job of cleaner? Petson said that he had brought someone. You look very young. Do you know anything?'

'I can clean and I work hard.' Malele felt self-conscious under the hard stare. 'I can do the work.'

'It is not difficult. Most women could do it. Reg card?'

'I have lost mine. I am waiting for another.' The lie came fluently.

'I don't suppose it matters. Mr Chona had better see you I suppose. He likes to know what staff we take on, even cleaners. Come with me.' She tossed the heavy braids of hair back and swayed off towards the office, Malele following.

'I don't like her perfume,' Malele told herself. 'I wouldn't use it.' But she wished she had the poise and the clothes of the secretary.

Mr Chona was disinterested. He sat behind his desk, his eyes, behind the gold-rimmed spectacles, flicking over Malele. 'She can start now, Sylvia. Just arrange salary and so on. Don't worry about the reg card for the time being. The last applicant didn't turn up and there is that big opening tomorrow so we need someone to clean and polish. This one will do, at least for now.'

He dismissed Malele with an abrupt nod of his head and

returned to his mobile phone. Sylvia led her out of the office. Depression came over Malele. Both the boss and the secretary had treated her as though she was nothing, then commonsense returned and she asked herself why they should treat her any differently. After all, a cleaner was a humble job and they obviously felt themselves to be superior. She asked diffidently if there was anywhere she could stay. Being with Eunice was fine, but she was only there until she could find a place of her own.

'There is a small room at the back. We like to have some staff on the premises and you will be expected to stay late sometimes if we have an opening in the evening. Part of your duties will be to wash up glasses and plates and help our regular staff. Start tomorrow and we will see how you do. Bring the reg certificate when it comes.'

Petson showed her the room. It was tiny and part of the old servant's quarters which now housed an old man who worked in the garden, and his wife. They would have to share the lavatory and the cold shower, but to Malele it seemed wonderful. A place of her own and a job. She would move in and in her daydreams, by sheer hard work, she would make such a success of it that she would one day become something more important than a cleaner.

'I am glad for you,' said Boniface when she told him the news. 'It was lucky that I heard about the job. I doubt if they will ever worry about the reg certificate. If you haven't got one they won't have to join any sort of pension fund for you. All that costs money and now you will be just an item on their expense account.'

Malele smiled. 'I won't care what I am. Thanks for finding me work. I have been feeling guilty at staying with you and your mother even though you have made me so welcome.'

'You have been welcome. I sometimes feel that I am poor company for my mother. She sees other men bring home

49

girls and then get married, but that is not for me. I am as I am, but because of this I prefer to remain alone.'

'But why? Many men like you marry and have children.'

'I am a poor twisted thing, Malele. Let us not pretend otherwise. To me, marriage is something for other people.'

There was no trace of self-pity in his voice, only an acceptance. 'These things happen and I am lucky to be working and to have my mother to care for me. She has given me so much and when she is old I will be able to help her. Long ago I decided that I would be single.'

'I can't see why. There must be plenty of girls who would like to go out with you.'

'But I would not like to go out with them, so there it is.'

Chapter 6

Malele arrived early at the gallery for her first day's work, her bundle of clothes in her hand. The gardener and his wife were cooking their food over a charcoal fire and the woman greeted her.

'So you are to have the small room? Well that is fine, but remember that we are a respectable place and we do not want an endless stream of boyfriends coming and going all night. What you do away from here is your own business, but here any noise and any bad behaviour will be bad for my husband and for myself.'

Malele was a bit startled by what she said. 'Amai, I am to live in the small room as you have said. I have no boyfriends who will visit me all night and I am a quiet person. I do know how to behave. My mother has brought me up well.'

'I hope so. Here is the key to the room. You will have to make your own food as I have enough to do for the two of us, my husband and myself.' Her small eyes peered at the bundle that Malele was carrying. 'Is that all you have? The room has no furniture so what will you do?'

'I will manage. I have a blanket and my friend has lent me a pot.' Malele was tempted to tell the woman that it was none of her business, but as she was to live next to the couple she decided to be polite and not to become angry.

'The last cleaner had friends all night. I wonder if you will really be any better.' The woman sat down beside the fire again.

Her husband nodded to Malele and smiled. 'Take no notice, mwana, Leah has a sharp tongue and the last cleaner upset her. Put your bundle in the room and then I will show you what you have to do. The rest come in later and it is a good thing to have everything clean before they get here.'

51

The room looked very small and bare and the window was dust-covered. Malele put the bundle down, noting that a bed mat had been left by the previous occupant and that the only furniture was a wooden chair which had seen better days.

'It's a start,' she said aloud. 'And it is mine. I'll manage.'

Amos, the gardener, let her into the kitchen and indicated where the brooms and the cleaning materials were kept. It was all strange to the girl and she struggled to remember the few domestic science lessons that she had had two years back. In the village it was a simple matter of sweeping and washing, but now she was faced with tins of polish and cleaning materials. She read the instructions on the tins and containers and started by sweeping the floor. It was very dusty and the corners of the room and the gaps between the cupboards had not been well cleaned for a long time. Malele got a bucket of water and by using a scrubbing brush managed to get them shining again. She was on her hands and knees when Sylvia Maunga, the secretary, came in. Malele got to her feet.

'Morning, Miss.'

The secretary ignored her greeting. 'At least you seem to be making the place a bit cleaner,' she said. 'The last woman was terrible. There are some maids' uniforms in the cupboard which should fit you. Use them when you are here. We want coffee brought to the office and to the gallery staff every morning at nine, and again at eleven hours, then in the afternoon at fifteen hours. The cups and the coffee are in the top cupboard, and there is cremora for the milk.'

She sounded brisk and efficient, but not friendly. Her hair was in a ponytail that morning and Malele noticed her elegant red fingernails. She glanced down at her own rough hands and once again vowed that one day she would be like Sylvia. In the meantime she was glad to wear the uniform as she had felt out of place in her chitenge cloth.

When Sylvia had gone back to her office, Petson

appeared. 'Hard at it? That's the girl. I bet Sylvia has been in and told you what to do, but is there anything that I can tell you? Do you know where everything is?'

'Coffee cups and something called crem something?'

'Top shelf there. The Cremora is what replaces the milk in our coffee and saves us having to send out for fresh milk. Convenience food.'

'Thanks. I haven't heard of it before. It is all a bit strange but I am learning fast.'

'That's the girl. Straight from the sticks but becoming civilized. Don't forget to bring my coffee at nine. I'll be finishing hanging the paintings and then you can come in and give the place a polish. We are having the opening tonight and everything needs to look good. You will be needed to help wash glasses and so on.'

He sauntered off.

'From the sticks indeed. He is too full of himself and I am not sure that I like him,' Malele muttered, but she realized that he had found her the job and that he was really her only friend at the gallery.

The day passed quickly. Malele swept and polished and had hardly time to look at the display of paintings being hung. She had seen some of them the day before, but now there were bright new ones decorating the walls. The artist, a young man with Rastafarian locks and grubby jeans, ignored her as he went round adjusting the pictures and arguing with Petson as to where each should go. Malele hardly dared to look at the work as she had so much cleaning to do. She finished the kitchen and the entrance hall, then started on the gallery.

'Hey, Malele, don't forget the coffee for the sculptor out in the courtyard. He is the only one there today,' Petson interrupted her polishing. 'The artists there have a cup each at eleven and it is past that time now.'

Malele put down her cloth and made a cup of coffee.

Placing it on a tray she went into the courtyard. 'Sorry that I am late,' she said as she handed the elderly sculptor his cup. 'I didn't know that I was meant to bring it to you.'

'Not a problem,' he said, his hands caressing the smooth curve of the wood.

'I hardly notice time when I am busy.'

Malele examined the sculpture. She had no idea what it was meant to be but the curves and texture of the wood pleased her and made her want to touch it. The man was watching her, a smile on his lips.

'Now ask what it is. Or do you have an idea?'

'None at all, but I like it and I don't know why. What is it?'

'An abstract idea of flight. See ... the curves all run upwards and if you think of a bird taking off the whole idea is to go soaring upwards. Some of the wood is smooth and polished, some rough and flight must be like that. Of course it is not finished and it is only my idea, but I am glad that you like it. I hope that someone with money will feel the same way and buy it.' He put three large teaspoons of sugar into the cup and said, 'Sugar for energy. This wood is hard and difficult to work.'

'I am sure that someone will buy it when it is finished. To me, it is beautiful.'

She worked until late afternoon, pausing to eat the buns that she had bought from a nearby seller.

'A clean uniform for this evening please,' Sylvia told her. 'The opening is at eighteen-thirty hours and you will be in the kitchen. The glasses will be brought through when they are used and you must wash them carefully and then dry them. The plates of snacks will be delivered at fifteen hours so be here to receive them. I suppose Petson will be here then and he can sign for them.'

Malele nodded. She was tired but the excitement of the opening was something to look forward to. She was alone in the kitchen when the hotel van drew up and a smart waiter brought in trays of food.

'You new?' he asked. 'Where is Petson? He usually signs for these.'

'He hasn't come back yet. I will sign.'

She checked the number of trays against the number quoted on the invoice and signed for them, scrawling her bold signature at the bottom of the page. The snacks looked delicious and Malele felt waves of hunger sweep over her. She had eaten little all day.

The hotel van drove off and Malele was alone again. There was no sign of Petson. Hunger overcame her and she took one small sausage roll from one of the trays and pushed it into her mouth. No one would notice if one roll was missing she thought, guilt almost overcoming her hunger. She rearranged the snacks so that the gap did not show. She heard Petson's footsteps and hastily wiped the crumbs from her mouth.

'Hey, I am late. I met a friend and stayed to talk. I see that the snacks have come. Did you sign for them?'

'Yes. The invoice is here. They cost so much ... will the gallery pay for them?'

'Sure. They always have the same order for an opening. Don't look so shocked. Things are expensive in town, but it is not our money so who cares? Come on, let's have one or two bits before the crowd arrives.'

'Are we allowed to?'

'Not really, but who will know.' Petson took several of the filled rolls and handed them to Malele, then ate some himself.

'Don't look so guilty. These snacks will be passed round the guests along with the wine and the few that we have won't matter at all. Now, I'd better get along and see that the wine is opened. Did you put the glasses on the table?'

'Yes. There are many there. The secretary showed me what was needed.'

'Fine. Come with me and bring some of the plates of food. They go on the long table. Here I'll take some.'

He opened several of the bottles of wine and told her to fill some of the glasses. 'Right, now some with the red. That's it. Fine. That should do for the time being. Sylvia and I will be taking trays of wine and food round, and people can help themselves too. Here, have a glass, red or white?'

'I have never tasted wine.'

'That's what the sticks do for you. Try the white, it is sweeter.'

Doubtfully, Malele took a glass and tasted the wine. It was disappointing and she would have preferred a Fanta, but Petson was watching her so she pretended to be enjoying it. She was back in the kitchen when the other gallery assistant, Michael, came in, followed by Sylvia.

'Where is Petson?' Sylvia asked. 'Is he here?'

'In the main gallery, Miss Maunga.'

'Good. I hope that he isn't sampling the wine. Go and see, Michael. Now you know what you have to do?'

She picked up the invoice from the table where Petson had left it. 'I see that you signed for the snacks. Why? Wasn't Petson here?'

'He was busy. I was in the kitchen, so I signed.'

'And did you think to check the delivery with the invoice?'

'I did. It was correct.'

'You have good writing. That surprises me as so many young people don't.'

The wine made Malele bold. 'I may come from the village but I have passed grade nine and I was head of the school.'

'Oh well, you won't have much opportunity to show off your education here.' Sylvia swept out of the kitchen leaving a trail of perfume, her smart patent leather shoes tapping on the polished floor. Michael reappeared grinning.

'What was she on about? I heard you standing up to her and saying that Petson was busy. She has it in for him these days; he was late more likely and I bet he has had a glass or two. Sylvia disapproves and thinks that only senior staff like her ought to have it before the show. Oh well, I won't get anything before the opening, that's for sure, with that dragon guarding the booze ... I usually get here in time to have some but I am late this evening.'

Malele wondered if the glass of wine was having an effect on her. Her head felt fuzzy and she was a little unsteady. She hoped that no one would notice and sat down on the kitchen chair. 'I shouldn't have had it or the rolls,' she thought in panic. 'I knew it was wrong and now if anyone notices I will lose my job and be out of work again.'

No one noticed and Malele washed and dried glasses and worked in the kitchen until the last of the invited guests had gone. She could hear the hum of voices and the taped music. Occasionally Michael or Petson brought in a pile of used glasses for her to wash.

From the kitchen she could catch glimpses of the guests as they passed by the doorway on their way to the washrooms. Some looked prosperous and were well-dressed but a few were in very casual clothes. Suddenly she saw someone that she recognized. He was the man who had stolen her money at the bus stop. For a moment she could not believe her eyes, then he was gone. Her heart was thudding with fright and anger as she waited for him to return along the passage. It couldn't be; it was too much of a coincidence and the gallery was not the place for him. Malele moved closer to the door to get a better view. He came down the dim passageway, dressed very much as he had been at the bus station. She had no idea of confronting him, but as he drew level with the doorway their

57

eyes met and she realized that he too had recognized her. She drew back. He paused for a second then went back into the main gallery without a backward glance. Malele retreated into the kitchen and sat down on the chair. The meeting was so unexpected and it brought back all the distress that she had suffered at the station. She had to find out who he was, so she waited for Petson to come in and asked him.

'Sounds like Angelo, but I'm not sure. There is plenty of that sort around tonight. They are mostly artists or relations of artists who get invited because they are part of the policy to mix the public with the actual artists and painters. Why do you want to know. I wouldn't have thought that Angelo would have set your heart fluttering. I hate to say it but he is a bad type and up to all sorts of things.'

'He hasn't, at least not in the way you mean.' For some reason she did not tell Petson what had happened with the money.

'I just wondered who he was as I had seen him before.'

'I expect that it is Angelo. Come with me and point the man out if he is in the gallery. Do you want to meet him?'

'No. It is just curiosity.' She followed Petson to the gallery entrance and saw the man across the room.

'There. That man in the red shirt. Talking to the woman in the green dress.'

'Oh, that's Angelo all right. He is Sylvia's brother and through her he has managed to show a few paintings in the gallery. Not that they sell well but she is trying to boost his career. That is what influence does. Without her he wouldn't get a look in, but because of her he has friends in the right places.'

'I see.'

Malele went back into the kitchen full of dismay. To have one of Sylvia's relatives in conflict with her was unexpected and although she knew that he had stolen from her, he could so easily say that she had accosted him at the bus station and his friend would laugh and support him. She tried to think what she could do but there was nothing and all she could do was to hope that the man would be too embarrassed to say anything and that he would not make trouble for her. She sighed. Life had so many complications.

By twenty-one hours there were only the gallery staff left. Mr Chona nodded to Malele as he passed the kitchen and Sylvia appeared with a half-full tray of snacks which had been left over. She placed it on the table.

'Here, Malele. I expect that you could do with something to eat. Take these leftovers as your supper. Tomorrow we will finish the clearing up and the cleaning. Now I am going to lock up and you can go.'

The day was over and Malele ate the snacks in her room. The single electric bulb showed up the bareness of the room, but Malele was too tired to notice or to care. The wine effect had worn off and she hoped that Sylvia hadn't taken offence at her speaking like that. 'I seem to lie all too easily these days,' she thought. 'Still it saved Petson from a bit of trouble. And maybe I should not have told her that I was head of the school. I was, but she may think I was boasting. Too late now. What is done is done. Tomorrow is another day. And the same goes for Angelo.'

She fell asleep on the bed mat, her blanket wrapped round her and over her head. Amos and his wife had turned out their lights and there was silence apart from some dog barking at shadows in the distance.

Chapter 7

The days passed. Malele became familiar with her duties at the gallery and began to make friends. Petson laughed and joked with her but Sylvia paid little attention to her. She sometimes went over the road to see Boniface during the lunch break and began to look forward to seeing him.

'Don't feel that you have to visit me,' he said as she sat with him eating a bun. 'I am sure that you have better things to do.'

'I want to see you. Don't think that I feel that I have to. Can't you ever realize that people do like you and that they come to see you because of that? I enjoy talking to you. I hate it when you feel sorry for yourself and think that you are different.'

'I am, but thanks for coming. I just didn't want you to feel that you had to or anything like that. You are good for me, Malele. You tell me what others don't and I am always glad to see you.'

Boniface listened to all the gallery gossip and Malele enjoyed telling him about her days there. 'Petson is nice but he seems just a bit too smart and careless. Sylvia would love to throw him out I think, but somehow he survives.'

'And that Angelo? Have you seen him again?'

'No, thank goodness and I don't want to, but I am sure that one day he will appear. He is the one bad thing about being at the gallery and I keep thinking of him.'

'What can he do? You are working there and it is none of his business. Forget it. He knows that he stole your money and he won't want that known.'

'It is only my say-so and his friend would say that I came up to Angelo at the bus station.' Malele shivered. 'He would say that I was a prostitute or something and then what would

60

Mr Chona think if he heard that? He is said to be a great church man and I am sure that he would hold it against me.'

'Stop worrying. Nothing will happen. Now it is time to go back to work.' Boniface struggled up and Malele crossed the road to the gallery hoping that he was right. She was too busy to really give it much thought.

The gallery was holding a workshop for artists. 'It happens every so often,' said Petson. 'Good for business in a way and it encourages artists. Good for the gallery image too as then the powers that be see that they are helping the local art world. This time we have one of the top artists from Zimbabwe coming to lecture and teach. Fifteen artists are coming to work. It should be interesting.'

'Don't you ever want to paint and to join in?' Malele asked. 'You have so much to do with art that I am surprised that you aren't an artist.'

'I have enough sense to know that I have no talent,' Petson told her. 'I did have a go and decided not to go on. I wish that I could really paint but I can't so I help arrange things for other artists instead. It's less work even if it is not so profitable as some paintings are. At least I get a regular salary which is more than most artists do.'

'Seems a pity all the same. I sometimes wish that I knew how to paint.

'Stick around, girl. Perhaps the lovely Sylvia may be persuaded to let you join a workshop one day. I see that her brother is enrolled for this one. If she didn't use her influence he wouldn't get anywhere. That is what nepotism is all about.'

Malele had no idea what nepotism was, but the thought of Angelo being in the gallery dismayed her. 'Hey, you are looking glum. What's wrong? Don't tell me that Angelo is part of your past ... a nice girl like you?'

'No. I didn't know his name until you told me who he was. I met him once before, that is all.'

61

'Seems he made a great impression, maybe not a good one. What happened?'

'Nothing. I don't like him, that's all.'

'Join the club. I don't either, but for the job's sake I don't tell him. Tactful, that's me, especially where my welfare is concerned. I'd advise the same for you. Sylvia has too much influence here and she loves him.'

'Thanks. I hope that I won't have anything to do with him.'

The workshop started and Malele was told to organise the mid-morning coffees and teas. She arranged the cups and the biscuits on a long table in the courtyard and as she poured, she listened to the end of the lecture given by the Zimbabwean artist. All the time she was conscious of Angelo sitting at the back of the courtyard.

'I will pretend that I don't recognise him,' she told herself. 'Then perhaps he will ignore me.'

The lecture ended and there was a rush to the table. Malele and Petson handed out cups and offered biscuits. Michael was one of the artists taking part in the workshop. Angelo was one of the last to come for coffee. He sauntered up to the table and placed himself squarely in front of Malele. She stared at him coldly.

'Ah, coffee. Put three sugars in for me, sweetheart, that's a good girl. Must keep up the old energy. Never know when I may need it.' He grinned at her. 'Come to think of it how about meeting me after this is over?'

'Here is the coffee. I have put in the sugar.'

'Thanks. How about outside the gate at seventeen hours? That maid's outfit does things for you ... nicer than the chitenge perhaps.'

Malele turned away, her hands shaking. 'No thank you. I am busy.' She saw Petson watching her.

'Too bad. There are other days and I will be around.' He let his eyes slide over her. 'Very nice and available too.'

Malele hated him and scowled. She would not even speak to him again. As he left, Petson asked what he had said that had made her so angry.

'Just trying to meet me, that's all.'

'I hope that you told him to get lost.'

'I did.' Malele tossed her head. 'He is awful and I can see him being a problem.'

'That's the penalty for being a good-looking girl. Someone needs to sort him out, but preferably not me.'

Malele had a vague feeling of disappointment at his words but she understood. He needed the job. The workshop would be over in a week so perhaps she could stay out of Angelo's way. But that was not possible. Angelo waited until Malele was alone in the kitchen and the rest of the artists were working.

'All alone? That's what I like to see. How about we go off to your room for a while? All this serious art is making me want a woman. I could hardly believe it when I saw you here, all dressed up as a maid.'

'Get out,' Malele hissed. 'And don't come back in here. I am not one of your prostitutes as you know very well. You stole my money at the bus station and then tried to accuse me of being a street-woman. You are a lying thief and I don't want anything to do with you. I haven't said anything about what you did, but I will if you don't go away.'

'Try it. Who is going to believe you? I even have a friend who saw you come up to me. I fancy you and if you are nice to me I will say nothing.'

'Get out.' Malele snatched up a pot and threatened to hit him.

Angelo caught hold of it and twisted it out of her hand.

'Naughty, naughty. Now, before I get angry, will you come with me or not?'

'No, no, no. You are a thief and a liar and I hate you.'

'You will be glad to have me one day. Remember that

jobs are hard to get and my sister is your boss. How would she feel if I told her about you accosting me? And Mr Chona is too pure to like it.'

Malele slapped his face with all the force that she could muster. 'Get out before I scream and say that you are trying to rape me.'

He stepped back, his eyes watering from the blow. 'You will be sorry for this. I like my women spirited but not like you.'

He left the kitchen and Malele sank into the chair and buried her face in her hands. Petson found her like this as he passed on his way to the toilet.

'What's the matter? You look like something bad happened.'

'Nothing. I am all right.'

Perhaps if she said nothing, Angelo would do the same and leave her alone. Malele spent as little time in the workshop as she could, but everyday there was coffee and tea to pour out and she had to organise the lunchboxes which were delivered from the hotel. Angelo was always present, watching her with a predatory expression and made a point of brushing against her if he happened to be close enough. Malele tried to ignore him. If he had not been there she would have listened to more of the lectures and talks that the Zimbabwean artist was giving, but even so she learned from him and was able to take a new and informed interest in the work that the various artists were doing. After the workshop ended each day she would go round the half-finished work and try to assess it on the strength of what she had learned. Petson found her there and nodded approvingly.

'I like to see people taking an interest. What do you think of this thing?' He pointed to a canvas. 'The artist is trying to make a composition of the market. The only trouble is that I think he is putting so much in, that now I find it a mess. Not that it matters much what I think, I will never be an artist, but I am learning what sells and what doesn't. Perhaps that means I know a good painting when I see it.'

Malele looked at the mass of colour and people. That morning, while she was pouring out the coffee, she had heard the lecturer say that a painting with too many bright colours all competing with one another would probably not succeed as every picture needed some neutral spaces of colour. It had stuck in Malele's mind because the man had made such a telling example that she remembered it.

'Think of a beautiful diamond pendant. It will look wonderful if it is against a plain background, but if it is against a wildly patterned fabric it will lose its impact and become just a part of the general pattern.'

Shyly, Malele reminded Petson of what had been said. 'Perhaps there is too much colour? But I don't know anything about painting, it's only what I heard at the talk.'

Petson said nothing for a moment. 'You know, you could be right. Funny how hard it is to understand what is wrong with things but I like to try. You must have really listened, Malele, and you could be quite correct. Now why didn't I think of that?'

'I had nothing to do but listen,' Malele said. 'I listen as much as I can and I wish that I could be an artist, but I don't think I could.'

'Why not, if you are so interested?'

'Well, one day, when I have the time and the materials then I might try. Who knows, I might surprise you all!'

'You might at that. For a village girl you do seem to be interested in things and you do learn.'

'Village girl! You also call me the girl from the sticks and that annoys me. I may come from the village but now I am in town and I will stay here.'

Petson laughed. 'I only do it to annoy you. That is how I am. I enjoy teasing people. I must like you because I was angry with Angelo for talking about you yesterday.'

He stopped as though he had said too much, then said seriously; 'Did you know Angelo before, Malele?'

'I only met him at the bus station. Why? What is he saying?' Malele had a cold feeling in her stomach. Angelo could do her so much harm and she so badly wanted him to stop thinking about her.

'Nothing that matters. He seemed to think that he knew you quite well. Don't worry about it. Angelo is always talking about people and no one listens.'

'Please tell me what he said. It does matter to me.'

'Oh, only that he gave the impression that ...' Petson paused and shifted uncomfortably.

'That what?'

'Well that ... once you and he had been close and ...'

'We have never been close. That is a lie and now let me tell you what actually happened.'

Malele told Petson about the incident at the bus station. 'That is what happened and he is a thief and a liar. I would never be close to him.'

'I am glad of that. From what he said I thought that he must have been told to push off by you and this is his way of getting back at you. What you have said is even worse. Never mind, the course will be over very soon and then he hardly ever comes here, except when he wants Sylvia to give him money or to find a buyer for his work.'

'Is he good?' Malele had to ask.

'Not very. Sylvia finds buyers and she gets his work into the gallery because of her working here and being able to do it. Angelo is slick and he knows how to please a client. Most of his things are bought by diplomat's wives who like to be patrons of art, even if they know very little. There are many better artists here.'

'I feel so bad now that I know he is talking about me.

Will he tell Sylvia? If he does she may decide to sack me.'

'This is man's talk ... you know the sort of thing that we say when we get together and a girl's name comes up. We do it to make other men think we are irresistible and it is a form of boasting really. It is not what one says to one's sister. Forget it, Malele. I told him to shut up and to stop telling stupid stories so he went off. I am sorry that I said anything. It sort of slipped out.'

'I thought that if I said nothing, the whole thing would go away. Stupid of me.'

'I told you to forget it. Forget it. No one pays any attention to that kind of talk and you mustn't worry. What he has said is like yesterday's news ... history and forgotten.'

'Not always.' Malele whispered. 'Just when I was so happy here. Now I expect people to be talking about me and the unfair part is that it is not true.'

'Stop worrying. It is not worth it. I know the truth and I will tell Angelo so.

The course ended and the workshop was over. Malele hated walking into the room where the artists were assembled and imagined that they were discussing her and laughing at her. She knew the sort of thing men said about girls they didn't like and she was sure that Angelo was well able to make her out to be promiscuous.

She told Boniface what had happened. 'That's people, Malele. I know that they talk about me and some of them think that my mind is as twisted as my body, but one gets hard and used to it. I know who I am and that is what matters. One day when I am a qualified accountant I will have a good job and then they will hold their tongues. In the meantime, I refuse to listen to them. You must do the same, and you must plan your future. You can't stay a kitchen-maid for ever, not if you want to have a career and to get somewhere. Think about it, Malele. Here you are having left your home for Lusaka and you have found work. That is fine, but what about in the future? You are grade nine, again that is fine, but are you doing anything to improve on that?'

'I expected more sympathy from you.'

'You have my sympathy for what it is worth, and my mother's too, I have no doubt, but sympathy is no good. It is up to you to work towards something. Perhaps, being a girl, you will marry and be content as a housewife and mother, but from what you have said I think you want more.'

'You know I do. I want to do something with my life, and if I ever marry and have children that will be on top of a career.'

As she spoke Malele realised that they were brave words but unless she did something soon she would drift along. She was young but time was passing. 'You are right but I don't know what I should do. I will think and when I see your mother I will ask her what she thinks too. I needed something to make me plan again. Now I will aim at something ... when I have decided what to do.'

Boniface patted her hand gently. 'Life is tough, Malele, even for pretty girls like you. Women probably have a harder time than men finding a career and they have the option of being married and kept by a man. My mother and I are your family now and we will be behind you, but only you can make a future for yourself. What about studying at night school? There are classes in various things after working hours. Getting there is a problem, and paying the fees, but let's think about what can be done.'

Chapter 8

'But I can't afford it,' Malele said.

She was sitting with Boniface and Eunice during a visit to their house one Sunday. Eunice was getting ready to go to the bus station to sell her food and Boniface had brought Malele a brochure which advertised a correspondence class for Grade Ten.

'You can't afford not to, Malele,' he said severely. 'Do you intend to remain in the gallery kitchen for ever? Look, I have a little saved and I'll pay for the course. You can pay me back when you can. Anyhow, by that time I'll be employed as an accountant and I'll have enough money not to need it.'

'No,' Malele shook her head. 'I'm not borrowing. But thanks all the same.'

'Then have the course as a gift from amai and myself. That way there is no repayment. You must get better grades and this is the only way.'

Malele thought for a long moment. She badly needed to get ahead and she realized that without at least a Grade Ten she would have little opportunity of a career.

'I couldn't take it as a gift. That would be totally wrong and I would be ashamed of myself for taking it. You are quite right about my needing the grades and if you will pay for this year I promise to repay you as soon as I can. I don't like doing this, but if you are sure that you can manage the money, I say thank you for the loan.'

'Done. And remember that there is no rush to repay me. One day I will be rich enough to buy you all the things that you want, one day when I am an accountant.'

She was startled by his words. What did he mean by one day and all the things that she wanted? Malele stared at Boniface, trying to see if he was serious or not. He met her gaze with an enigmatic smile and a shrug of his shoulders.

'A manner of speaking that's all. Now, let's plan for your future. You must write to your old school for a certificate saying that you have passed grade nine. There shouldn't be a problem as the teacher knew you and your family and must know what happened. Otherwise your mother would have to collect the paper, but if you ask nicely I expect that he will send the thing. Then you enroll and work begins.'

Lying awake that night, Malele wondered if she had made a mistake in taking the loan. Boniface and his mother had little enough and she was afraid that Boniface might think that she would be under an obligation to him. 'Stupid,' she told herself. 'He was only joking and he is not interested in girls anyway. He is always saying that he is a cripple. Anyway I will work so hard that I will pass quickly and then I can think about the next grades and a career.' Firmly she pushed any doubts away.

She pictured herself as a well-dressed secretary like Sylvia or perhaps as an office manager or a successful saleswoman. In each dream she was smart and beautiful and she had the world at her feet. She had to accept that getting there would be hard and sometimes she would wish that she had never started, but she was determined to get somewhere. Never mind the loneliness and the hard work, that was the price of success.

Once she was enrolled in the correspondence course, Malele worked hard, sitting in her small room night after night under the solitary lightbulb and studying the grade ten subjects, then writing out the answers and comments that she was to mail to the college. Some nights she almost gave up. She was tired and alone and she thought longingly of reading one of the magazines that Petson occasionally produced or simply going to sleep. Everything was too slow and too difficult. Then she would think of the future and of her ambitions and work harder than ever. Getting her grade nine certificate had not proved too difficult as the headmaster had decided to let her have it without her mother collecting it and it had arrived through the post. The national registration card had proved harder to get, and Sylvia kept asking when Malele would get it.

'No problem,' said Petson cheerfully when Malele confided in him. 'All they want is some relative to come with you and declare that the information is true. I'll be a relation. Just give me the details and we will be off to the boma. They take the photos and you pay them the fee.'

'I have saved the fee.' Malele was relieved that Petson was so confident. She had told him about running away and faking her age when she applied for the job.

'What's a year more or less? When you are ageing you will be sorry that you have to add a year, but that time is a long way off. Stop worrying. There is nothing criminal in this. Just force of circumstance and you look eighteen anyway so no one will query things. Why should they? Hundreds of people apply for reg cards every week and you will be just one more name.'

He went with her to the registration office and stood in the long queue. Together they filled in the application forms. Name of father, name of chief, name of village.

'The village isn't the same as the one on your reg card,' the official said severely, giving Petson a hard look. 'Are you sure that you are a cousin?'

Malele could feel her knees trembling. She needed this card so badly and now there was this query.

'Sure I'm sure, man. I'm her cousin all right, and when her father died, the mother took her to our village, but she was born where I said. You know how things are, parents die, families move, but the place of birth remains the same.'

'And your mother?' The man peered at Malele. She forced herself to meet his eyes. 'That is the problem. My

71

mother and my father have died and this man is my only relative. That is why he is here.'

'It will have to be checked, a pity that the birth certificate got burnt. So many seem to,' the man grumbled, then he shrugged. 'Give me the forms and the money, then come back in two weeks time after you have had the photograph taken.' The official wrote out a receipt for the money and turned to the next person, ignoring Malele and Petson.

'Right, come on cousin. We will be back.' Petson led the way out.

'I thought that he was going to be difficult,' Malele said as they reached the door. 'What if he checks with the chief and finds that my mother is still alive? Petson, just say he does? Will I go to prison?'

'Nah, nothing like that. He won't check and this time in two weeks you will have your card. Stop worrying. Do you really think that he is going to all that bother? He gets paid and that is all he cares about. You are a year older than you should be but so what. Your birth certificate is most likely lost anyway and so many people don't have them anyhow. Stop worrying, girl from the sticks. This is the city and you are a minor detail in the life of it. Nothing will happen and if one doesn't seize opportunities, one never gets anywhere. Just think, if you hadn't had the savvy to run away, you would have been married to that old man. God helps him who helps himself. Remember that.'

As they went out of the door, a man hailed Petson, shouting across the queues. 'Hello there, my brother. What brings you here? I saw your sister last week. She sends you greetings and says that the family is waiting for you to go on leave and see them.'

Petson chatted for a moment, then went on. Malele was waiting for him.

'Oh Petson, that man said that he had seen your sister and

72

the family were waiting. You told the Reg man that you were the only one left of the family. Do you think he heard? Will he remember that and when we go for the reg card make some trouble?' She was nervous and worried.

'Of course not. Once we had left the counter we were out of his mind. Anyway there is always the extended family to account for things like that. I might be your only true relative. He doesn't know. Nothing will go wrong. Lots of cards are got this way and who cares?'

'I always seem to be telling lies these days,' Malele said ruefully. 'There was a time when I was very truthful.'

'Part of growing up. We all do it to survive. Some lies don't matter at all.'

'But some do.'

'Then, if it is very important, don't lie. This is called a white lie ... note the
white! It is like saying that you are well when you are ill and things like that.'

Malele remained silent. Petson had a very convenient conscience about lies and she was benefiting from them. She felt a little ashamed, but consoled herself that she was doing no one any harm.

He was right. Two weeks later Malele had her national registration card and Sylvia remarked tartly that she was beginning to wonder if Malele would ever get one. 'At least you are legal now,' Sylvia said.

'Sylvia is looking like thunder,' Petson reported one morning as he settled into the kitchen chair. 'I don't know what has bitten her but it must be serious. Not that she is ever sweetness and light unless she gets a rise or a new boyfriend. They don't last too long either.'

Malele was washing the kitchen floor, down on her hands and knees with a bucket of water beside her. 'I don't see her much. When she wants something she comes in and tells me, but otherwise she is in the office most of the time and I clean it before she gets here.'

'Probably something to do with that brother of hers. I hear that he has been out with expensive girls and that means money problems. Not had any more trouble with him, have you Malele? He has a foul tongue and that is for sure. Michael and I gave him a hard time over things he was saying about you after the workshop.'

'I know and thank you both for that. I keep hoping that he will forget all about me. I haven't seen him for a while which is great.'

'I expect he is too busy elsewhere,' said Petson cheerfully. 'He's a bad lot and Sylvia defends him. Nice loyal sister but what a waste on someone like Angelo.'

The next morning as Malele was cleaning Sylvia's office the secretary came in and sat down at her desk.

'Good morning Miss Maunga,' Malele smiled at her, hurrying to finish dusting the filing cabinets.

Sylvia did not reply and sat looking down at her desk. Then, with an effort she said 'Malele, you clean here each morning don't you?'

'Yes.'

'Last week did you happen to open any of my drawers?' Malele looked at her in surprise.

'No, I never open the drawers. I only dust and polish the floor.'

'I thought not. Are you sure that you didn't find one of the drawers open and then shut it?'

'No. They are always shut and I get on with my work.'

'Are you sure?'

Malele felt her temper rising. 'I am sure. I have never found a drawer open. If I had I would have mentioned it to you and left it as it was. Why?'

'Never mind. I was only asking and you have given your

answer. Please hurry up with the dusting. I have a lot of work to get through.'

Malele finished her cleaning and went back into the kitchen. Petson was there waiting for her to make him a cup of instant coffee.

'Hey, you look like something has gone wrong. What's up?'

"Nothing, only Sylvia kept asking if I had found one of her desk drawers open and if I looked into her drawers. I haven't and I don't, but from the way she looked she thought that I had. Why?'

'No idea. Perhaps something has gone missing. That is all I can think of. Did she say anything else?'

'Just for me to hurry up as she had lots of work to do.'

'Ignore her. Now what about the coffee?'

'Help yourself if you are in so much of a hurry.'

'Now, don't be like that. It tastes so much better from your sweet hands. Besides, that is what women should do ... wait on the men.'

Malele's bad mood cleared as she laughed. Petson was impossible but he cheered her up and was a good friend. She was enjoying being part of the gallery and by being willing to take on extra work and by showing an interest, she was being given more responsibility. Mainly by Petson, she reminded herself. Mainly to save him work, but I am learning about pictures and hanging them, and a little about exhibitions.

She was cleaning the windows in the gallery entrance when she heard someone speaking from Sylvia's office and recognized Angelo's voice. He had been at the gallery recently, but she had managed to avoid him and now her first instinct was to retreat from the hallway. It was only the mention of her own name that made her pause and listen.

'That is nonsense,' Angelo said angrily. 'Do you really think that I, your brother, would steal your money? It is much

75

more likely to be one of the staff. What about that kitchen cleaner? She is nothing but a tart anyway, as I have told you, and who knows how honest she is?'

'Nothing is impossible, but on past history I would say that it was more likely to be you. I hear that you have a new and expensive girlfriend and you were also in the office the day the money went. Angelo, this is the last time I am warning you. Don't try things on me. I won't support you any longer and the next time I will call in the police.'

'And find the real thief. Look well about you, my sister, and don't blame me.'

'I will be more careful where I put an envelope of money. Now leave me. I have no money to give you and you will have to manage on your own in future. I am tired of helping you and I have too little myself.'

Malele heard a chair scraping back as she hurried into the kitchen and closed the door. How dare he say that she was a tart who stole money. She banged the tea-cups down on the tray as she dried them. He was a thief all right. That she knew all too well. His remarks made her feel dirty and disgraced and she hated him. Even through her anger, she felt a wave of sympathy for Sylvia at having such a brother and a sense of relief that Sylvia had not accepted that she had taken the money. The remarks of the previous week made sense now. Sylvia had been referring to money which had gone from her drawer. She heard the front door slam and knew that Angelo had gone.

'That is what happened,' Malele told Petson later. 'I bet Angelo took the money and then tried to blame me. I do wish that he would leave town and go somewhere far off.'

'Not a hope, unless the police get wise to him and he has to go. Sylvia is far too useful for him to leave. One day things will go wrong for him. They always do for these wide boys.'

'And I hope that I am there to see it. I will be so happy.'

'Forget it. Now come on, finish in the kitchen and come and help in the gallery. I have to get the new display up alone otherwise.'

Malele followed him and together they arranged the exhibition of new paintings on the walls. As they were working Mr Chona came in and stood watching them. Malele wondered nervously if he would mind her being there instead of in the kitchen, but he smiled and remarked that it was good to see her taking an interest in the work of the gallery.

'Do you enjoy looking at art works?' he asked.

'Yes, I do, but I don't know much about them. Only what I have learned here.'

'Keep learning. Art can bring such a lot into one's life. Get to understand it. Too few people take the time to do that, but owning a good work of art is a great pleasure.'

Chapter 9

Malele looked at the box of coloured pencils. The words Caran d'Ache were emblazoned across the front of the box and as she lifted the lid she could see the half-used pencils. Tentatively she took out a cobalt blue and ran the point over a piece of paper, scribbling the colour to widen the line. The blue was pale and the texture of the paper showed through. Malele licked her finger and moistened the colour. It sprang into brilliance and she rubbed her finger over it, spreading the blue into a transparent wash. She added a cadmium yellow, moistened the colour and watched as the yellow turned the blue into a green whenever the two colours met.

'Just as they said at the workshop,' she mused, remembering what the lecturer had said about colour mixing. 'Red, blue and yellow are the primary colours in a colour wheel and if you mix red with blue you get violet, blue with yellow makes green and yellow and red makes orange.'

She had listened to several of the workshop talks during her time at the gallery and after the most recent workshop she had found the coloured pencils stashed away in a cupboard. No one seemed to know who owned them and Petson remarked that they had been there for ages so who ever did own then had lost them.

'Not many people use Caran d'Ache. They are coloured pencils which can be moistened and then they are a bit like watercolours. I can't think who left these. Chuck them at the back of the cupboard and if someone claims them they will be there, but I doubt if anyone will.'

'I'd like to try them,' Malele thought. 'I know nothing about doing pictures but I would like to have a go. Do you think that I could try? Would anyone mind?' She said nothing aloud. She would probably be useless at art and she did not want anyone to see her failure.

The next day she took the crayons out of the cupboard and unseen, had carried them to her room. She also took a piece of cartridge paper that someone had abandoned after an attempt at figure drawing. The other side was clear and would do to draw on. For an hour she struggled with the colours, trying to make a picture of a market scene. She imagined old Eunice crouching over her fire and the people coming to buy the food, but her figures were deformed and their hands like bunches of bananas. The only good thing was that the colours were bright and when she half shut her eyes and hardly saw the clumsy figures, the picture was full of glowing colour.

'It's a mess,' Malele muttered as she pushed the paper away. 'I hoped for so much and look at it. The figures are hopeless.' Stubbornly she refused to give up. Turning the paper over she studied the rough sketch on the other side. The artist had drawn a man standing with one arm raised and Malele realised that it was a great deal better than her effort. She took a pencil and copied the drawing. Phrases from workshop lectures came back to her.

'The head goes roughly six times into the height of the body in an adult. The waist is two head lengths below the chin.'

She filled the paper with drawings and in the end she felt that she had learned a little about drawing a figure. It was getting late and she still had work on her correspondence course to do, but Malele felt that the time spent on the drawing had been worthwhile. Whenever she had time she practised with the crayons, using bits of rejected paper from the gallery and each day learning something more.

'If I live to be a hundred I will be quite good,' Malele giggled to herself. 'This is a slow process and I wish I could do more. I know what I want to do but somehow what I put on the paper isn't at all the same.'

Suddenly she felt depressed and lonely. Through the thin walls she could hear the murmur of the old gardener talking to his wife and the sound of their radio. She thought of her mother and of her grandmother and the life in the village. Had she made a mistake in leaving all that? Then she remembered the old man who would have married her and her depression lifted. Anything was better than that. In another year she would have completed Grade Twelve and then she could somehow manage to go to a secretarial college and learn to be a secretary. She pictured herself, poised and elegant, sitting behind a desk, answering the telephone and organising her boss's timetables exactly as she had seen Sylvia do. Life wasn't so bad. She had friends like Eunice and Boniface and Petson and at least she was earning a regular wage and even managing to save a little. Malele shook herself.

'Nothing happens without hard work and sticking to one's path,' she said aloud. 'Don't look back, keep going.'

There was a new exhibition scheduled for the next week and even Sylvia was excited about it. She seldom chatted to Malele, but this time she had told her that a woman called Irene Selassie was showing jewellery that she had made.

'She is from the Diplomatic Corps and comes from Ethiopia,' Sylvia said. 'I have seen some of her work and just wished that I had more money and could afford some of the things. The necklaces are beautiful and so are the bracelets, but of course they are right out of my price range. A pity as I would have looked good in them.'

When Malele saw the things being put out for display she agreed. There were heavy chains of silver and elaborately decorated earrings, all distinctively African and Malele found herself wishing that she too could afford them. Petson was helping Irene set up the work when Malele brought in the coffee and introduced her to the artist.

'They are so beautiful,' she said. 'I am sure that everything will sell on the first night. There must be so many women with money who will buy them.'

'I hope so. A lot of the influences come from my home in Ethiopia. Some of the pieces that I have used are old and quite valuable in a small way. I decided to use them as part of the necklaces and as pendants. They were just in a box and not being used so it is better to let others enjoy them. Then there are the silver and semi-precious stones. I have been here for only a short time and this is the first exhibition I have had in Zambia.'

'I wish you luck.'

Malele watched as the two pinned necklaces to cloth-covered display units and Irene made Petson redo anything that she didn't feel was quite right. He raised his eyebrows at Malele and gave a small grin as he redid things. Irene was very exacting and Malele laughed to herself at the hard time Petson was having. He was so used to dictating to artists about hanging their pictures that this was a new experience for him. Irene certainly had the upper hand.

'Hey, girl from the sticks, this is a job for a woman's fingers,' Petson said, dropping pins and struggling with an elaborate chain. 'Here, you will do this better than I can. You don't mind do you Irene? She will help. I have to go out to arrange some other things.'

'She couldn't be clumsier than you are,' Irene said sweetly, giving him a smile. 'In fact I am sure that Malele will be fine. Come on, Malele, we have a lot to do before the opening.'

Malele enjoyed the work and soon learnt how to show the jewellery off to its best advantage. Irene nodded her approval.

'You are doing fine. We have nearly finished. Thanks for the help. Poor Petson was all thumbs when it came to this sort of work. So many men are hopeless when it comes to delicate things.'

There was the usual excitement of the exhibition opening. Malele was used to this now and helped with the wine and the snacks. People kept arriving and a mixture of expensive perfumes pervaded the gallery. Diplomatic cars drove up to the entrance and well-dressed men and women got out, then the car drove off to wait until the show was over. There were many of the Apamwamba, the richer Zambians. There were also some old men with bright skinny girls with them. 'Not their wives,' Petson murmured. 'Sugar daddies will buy their girlfriends something for services rendered I expect.' Mr Chona was greeting people and Sylvia was speaking to the guests, her hair in an elaborate ponytail.

Malele kept an eye open for Angelo, but she did not see him. It was easy enough to miss him in the crowd which listened to the speech by the Minister of Culture opening the show and then exclaimed over the jewellery, but as the evening wore on she decided that he was absent. She relaxed and began to enjoy herself even though she was not really part of the crowd. By closing time there were red tags on many of the articles indicating that they had been sold. As the last guest left, Mr Chona locked up the gallery and told Petson to tidy there in the morning. Malele had removed all the uneaten snacks and the used glasses to the kitchen and had washed up as much as she could.

Petson and Malele ate what they wanted of the leftovers, discussing the people who had been there, Petson commenting on who was with who. He drained the last bottle of half-used wine.

'Time for bed. These late hours are killing me! Not the late hours, the early start. That is the problem. I would love to stay out to all hours, then sleep all morning.'

'See you at eight,' Malele teased, then took the rest of the leftovers out to the security guard who was on duty in his kiosk by the front gates.

'A good evening,' Petson remarked as she came back. 'Lots of sales and the buyers will collect at closing time tomorrow. Mr Chona is security minded with this lot. That's why he has taken the gallery key. Personally I doubt if anyone would bother to steal but one never knows. Come on, let's go home. I'll lock up the front door and you have the back door key.'

It was late when Malele got to bed. There was no time to study or to draw that night and she slept heavily, waking when it was almost time for work and she had to hurry. She had finished cleaning the kitchen and the hall when Petson arrived and they sat in the kitchen drinking coffee as they waited for Mr Chona to open the gallery room. They heard Sylvia come in and go to her office, her high heels clicking on the parquet floor.

'I'll take her coffee,' Malele said. 'I expect she would like some.'

She had made a point of looking after Sylvia in little extra ways ever since she had overheard the conversation between Angelo and his sister. At least Sylvia hadn't accepted Angelo's suggestion that Malele was a suspect and she was grateful.

'Thanks,' Sylvia said. She was busy painting her nails a brilliant pink and the smll of nail polish remover was thick in the office. 'It went well last night didn't it?'

She waved her drying nails in the air. 'I almost envied some of those girls getting presents from their sugar daddies!' she laughed. 'As soon as Mr Chona comes in you must get on with the gallery cleaning. It opens in an hour and a half and I see from the paper that the reporter has praised the show. That means plenty of people will come today.' She handed Malele the paper cautiously, keeping her still wet nails from being spoiled.

Malele read the review and nodded. 'It's a good one. Miss Selassie must be pleased with the sales. There seemed to be a lot of red tags on her things.'

'Well over half when I last counted and today others will come and buy.' She opened the window wide. 'Get the smell out of here before the boss comes. Now to work.' She dismissed Malele abruptly.

Mr Chona unlocked the gallery door when he arrived and went in with Malele and Petson to make sure that everything was all right. It was cold in the room with the air conditioning and there was the inevitable debris lying about from the crowd. Cigarette stubs lay in ashtrays or scattered on the floor, and discarded catalogues were strewn untidily over the tables. Malele started to clear up, thankful that she had done most of the hard work the night before. She retrieved a glass from the windowsill and scraped a smoked salmon canapé off the floor before she began dusting.

'Petson, you helped put out these things. Come over here. Isn't something missing from this display board?' Mr Chona sounded anxious.

Petson went over and thought for a moment. The display had a gap in it, but some of the things had been deliberately left with space round them to allow them to be seen better.

'Yes, I am sure that there was the big necklace with the silver cross. Malele, you know what went where in the end.'

Malele took one look and knew that the necklace she had so much admired had gone. 'Yes, and if you look carefully you can see where the pins have been pulled out. I helped put the necklace there and now there is a space.'

The only sign that something had been taken was a small tear where the necklace had been ripped off the board.

'I am sure I saw it myself just before closing time,' Mr Chona said in distress.

'It was there all right. I went round before I locked up. I was tired and I had already made a proper check earlier on, so I have to admit that I didn't check all that carefully right at the end. The thief has been clever in not leaving too obvious gaps.'

He was repeating the phrases as he stared at the display. There were still some amethyst earrings and a pendant there, a small display in themselves unless one knew what had been there before.

'I reckon there are three more gone,' Petson announced

from the other side of the room. Mr Chona and Malele hurried across.

'And I think there are some earrings missing too from here, and some of the silver things. There are spaces that should have something in them, I am sure.'

'Get the catalogue and check each item,' Mr Chona ordered. 'Sylvia, Sylvia, come here.' He was wringing his hands. 'This has never happened before in all the years I have had the gallery. And it had to happen now, at this exhibition. Sylvia, come here.'

Sylvia came in. 'What's the matter?'

'Look. Some of the jewellery has gone. One of the best necklaces and some of the silverware.' Petson waved the catalogue at her. 'Take this and do a check. I have been round once but you double check. I saw that everything was in order a few minutes before the end of the exhibition. Everything was there then as far as I could tell.'

'And Mr Chona locked up after everyone had gone. Are any of the windows broken or any signs of a break-in?' Sylvia sounded shocked and upset.

'Can't see any, but I will get the police here as soon as possible.'

Mr Chona hurried out to ring the Charge Office and the others looked at each other in dismay. It was unsettling to know that a thief had been at the exhibition.

'It must have happened at the very end of the evening,' Petson said. 'There is no sign of a break-in so someone must have taken the things while people were still here.'

'Impossible,' Sylvia snapped. 'We would have seen them.'

'Well, what else do you suggest? Mr Chona locked up and he has the only key so what else could have happened?'

'Whoever did it must have been so quick,' Malele said. 'I suppose that it could have been done when all of you were seeing people off and I was in the kitchen.'

'Maybe, and unless one checked carefully it probably wouldn't have been noticed at first. Not at a casual glance.'

'Whatever is Miss Selassie going to say?'

'Heaven knows and she is a tough lady. She was here until just before we locked up and she obviously didn't see anything wrong. The gallery has insurance which is lucky, but this is the first time we have shown any sort of jewellery. Usually it is pictures or sculpture or something like that with no real resale value for a thief.'

'Some of the stolen pieces had already been bought and paid for,' Sylvia remarked. 'That makes things even worse.'

'It certainly does.'

'The police are taking their time.'

'No transport as usual I expect,' Petson complained.

'They never have transport when they need it.'

'I can hear a land rover,' Malele said. 'That must be the police. I wonder what they will find?'

'Not much I expect, but at least they have arrived.'

They waited in silence as Mr Chona clattered down the front steps to greet them.

Chapter 10

The police came into the gallery, filling the room with their presence. Mr Chona ushered them into the gallery, his face anxious and unhappy. He showed them the places where the jewellery was missing.

'Whoever did it was smart,' said the tall detective sergeant examining the board. 'There are things still left here and unless one knows, it would be easy to think that the display was complete. The same with the other things. Is this very valuable stuff?'

'Not in world terms,' Mr Chona said. 'The stones are semi-precious and the real value lies in the few old artefacts and the workmanship. Still, I reckon that even in an underground market, the thief would get a few million kwacha for it and the silver could be melted down easily enough.'

'Even a few million kwacha is desirable if one has nothing. Have any of you any suspect in mind? Anyone who you think might have taken these articles?'

Malele was tempted to name Angelo but she said nothing. After all there was no reason to suspect him even though he was a thief. He had not been at the opening.

Taking over Mr Chona's office, the police interviewed everyone one by one. Malele gave them her particulars and explained what she had seen and done the night before. It was little enough and she was soon allowed to go. Sylvia and Mr Chona were sitting in the secretary's office and she and Petson retired to the kitchen.

'Isn't it silly,' she said to Petson. 'I felt quite guilty even though I knew nothing
at all. I suppose the police make one feel like that.'

'A common experience,' he assured her. 'I have to stop myself from being cocky with them ... purely defensive, but being a smart-ass doesn't impress them at all.'

'You sound as though you have had plenty of experience with police?'

'No, but in my misspent youth I got caught up with them once or twice, mainly on somewhat drunken sprees at parties. Nothing too bad at all and no repercussions. You know, if I didn't know that Angelo hadn't come last night I would have wondered about him.'

'Me too, but that would have been unfair. I enjoyed last night because he wasn't there.'

A uniformed constable came through the kitchen from the backyard, followed by Amos and Leah, the gardener and his wife.

'Wait there. You will have to be interviewed,' the constable told them as he went out again.

Malele smiled at her neighbours. She saw little of them, but occasionally stopped to chat if they were outside their house when she came off duty. Amos was always pleasant, but Leah still made little effort to be friendly beyond exchanging greetings.

'What has happened?' Amos asked.

'Someone has stolen some of the jewellery from the exhibition,' Malele explained. 'That is why the police are questioning all of us.'

'There were lots of people here last night,' Amos remarked. 'They will have a job trying to find the thief.'

'I expect so, but they are trying. I have already been in to give my statement and it isn't a problem. The sergeant was quite kind and it didn't take long.' Malele thought that Leah was apprehensive and wanted to comfort her. 'They only asked what I had seen and then my name and so on.'

'That's enough. I have no time for getting mixed up with the police. As far as I am concerned they are no better than the criminals,' Leah said firmly. 'I don't know what things are coming to; Amos and I being mixed up in things like this. And don't you go talking to them, Amos. Let them get on with things by themselves. Not that we know anything except that there was the usual noise and comings and goings that happens at all openings.'

Petson laughed. 'Come on, mama. They are only doing their duty and they don't like you any better than you like them I expect. Just answer what they ask you and that will be all.'

Leah gave him a baleful glare. 'Smart young man aren't you? As far as the police are concerned I will do what I have to and that is that. Police indeed! Never there when they are needed and there when they aren't. That is my experience of them.'

The constable came back, calling for his companion who was in the front of the building. 'Come round to the servants' quarters,' they heard him say, and listened to his retreating footsteps.

'I wonder what he has found,' Malele said.

'A full dustbin,' Petson quipped and Leah scowled at him.

'He was wandering round our yard,' she complained. 'I could see him through the window here. Nosing about, I have no doubt.' But he had found something and after a brief consultation in Mr Chona's office, the detective sergeant came through the kitchen with him and went down the back steps. Malele watched them go round to her side of the quarters, then they disappeared behind the building.

A few minutes later they reappeared, the sergeant holding something in his hand. Reaching the kitchen he held out an amethyst and silver earring. It lay like a fragile butterfly in his big hand. 'Is this from the exhibition?' he asked.

Petson and Malele stared at it, then simultaneously agreed that it was part of the exhibit.

'Where did you find it?' Petson asked.

'Outside the young ladies' quarters. Someone must have dropped it there.

Please come with me, miss, and let me see if there is anything else inside. I also want to look in your rooms.' He jerked his head at Leah and Amos. Malele felt her stomach lurch.

'I will come with you,' she said as calmly as she could.

'There is nothing in my room I am sure.'

'Let's look. You two come as well.'

Feeling like a prisoner, Malele accompanied the police to her room and unlocked the door. The little room looked pathetically bare and the single light barely dispelled the shadows.

'There you are,' she said. 'Look as much as you like. There is very little there so it won't take you long.'

She could feel Petson behind her and was grateful for his support. She watched as the police turned the bed mat and her few possessions over and shook out the box of crayons onto the floor. The pile of drawings lay on the chair and they too were scattered in the search.

'Nothing here,' the sergeant announced at last. 'Pick up your things and go back to the kitchen. We will go to the other quarters.'

Sullenly, Leah and Amos followed him and Malele and Petson were left alone to collect up the scattered things.

'Hey, Malele, I didn't know that you had the crayons and were working,' Petson said, holding up a sketch of a market. 'How long have you been doing this and why didn't you tell me. It is always good to have a critical eye on things.'

'They aren't good.' Malele took the sketch from him and added it to the pile she had. 'And I didn't ask permission to use the crayons because I wanted to try on my own and not have to make a public fool of myself.' She spoke defiantly. 'I know I shouldn't have borrowed the crayons, but you said that they had been there for ages.'

'So they had, and no harm done, but you aren't bad for a beginner, even though I say it and I am no artist.'

'Well, thanks, Petson. Now we had better get back to the

house. I hated them going through everything. It made me feel dirty.'

'Well, they found nothing so don't worry about them.'

But she did worry. The detective called her in again after he had finished with Leah and Amos. Leah was angry at the search which had uncovered nothing and was abrupt with the man. Amos tried to be placatory, but it was obvious that they were rated low on the list of possible suspects.

'Now, Miss Simonga. What do you know about the earring found just outside your door? It seems a funny place for it to be without you knowing about it. Didn't you see it this morning when you went out? It was right by the step.'

'No. I didn't see it. I was late in waking up and was in a rush. If I had seen it I would have picked it up, wouldn't I?'

'Perhaps, but it might have been dropped later?'

'Could be. How should I know? I didn't see it. That is all I can say?'

' Yes, but how did it get there in the first place? It is an odd place to find it unless someone was carrying things out of your room and dropped this by mistake. It is not as though it was on a path leading somewhere.'

Malele felt anger rising in her. The man was unreasonable and almost mocking. 'I can only say I don't know anything about it and that I didn't see it.'

'You are sure that you didn't have the jewellery in your room and then gave it to someone?'

'Of course I didn't. Why should I steal like that? I don't steal and you have no right to even suggest that I had the things.'

'It would have been easy for you to take them and then pass them on. After all you were the one who knew exactly how the items were pinned to the boards so you could take them off quickly.'

' Rubbish. I am sick of listening to you saying things like that. I did not steal

91

the jewellery and I did not see the earring. Can't you understand that?' She knew that it was unwise to get angry and that she must be careful what she said, but for a moment she didn't care. 'Look somewhere else for the thief. I know nothing.'

'We shall see. Now don't go away. Wait in the kitchen until I tell you what is happening.'

Malele found Petson waiting in the kitchen. Malele burst into tears when she saw him. 'They almost accused me of taking the things,' she sobbed. 'Why? I know that they found the earring almost on my doorstep, but anyone could have dropped it there. I wish that I had seen it and thrown it over the wall. Then all this wouldn't have happened.'

'Malele, listen. I think that there is more to this than just finding the earring. I heard Sylvia saying to Mr Chona that she had lost money before and she mentioned your name. Perhaps she said it to the police.'

Malele sat up abruptly. 'What? How could she? She was the one who didn't agree with Angelo when he suggested me. Why should she change now?'

She was shaking. Everything was piling up on top of her and there was nothing that she could do to stop it.

'Easy, girl from the sticks. This is only what I think and anyway there is no proof at all. No doubt the police will play about with fingerprints, but all of ours will be likely to be on the display boards as well as much of the public. Don't get upset. I know it is awful, but they are only doing what they are paid to do and once they realise that you have nothing to do with the theft, they will bully someone else. A pity that it isn't Angelo. That would be well deserved.'

Malele was grateful to him for his common sense. His words made everything seem less drastic and she wiped her eyes with the back of her hand.

'I just can't believe it about Sylvia. I know she thinks that

I am way beneath her but I thought that we were friendly enough and now this.'

'I had to tell you. It is better to know how people are than to go on trusting them, but she probably only mentioned it to Mr Chona. That is what I heard, nothing to the police.'

The police asked Malele to accompany them to the central police station. It was not a request. She had to go so she climbed into the back of the land rover and they drove off. She could see Petson and the others standing in the hallway watching her go. They drove in silence, Malele seated between two constables and soon reached the charge office.

Malele was frightened. Nothing that she could say seemed to make the police believe her and after three hours of questioning she was tired. All through the questioning she had denied that she had anything to do with the theft, even when she had been reduced to tears. 'I know nothing about it,' she kept repeating.

'I didn't even know that the earring was by my door. I told you that I was in a hurry this morning and I didn't see it. If I stole it, what have I done with the rest of the things?'

'Handed them to your accomplice. That is when the earring got dropped.'

'That's a lie. I didn't steal and I have no accomplice.'

'That is your story and we don't believe you. Now tell us the truth. You did steal the jewellery didn't you? We know that you did so you might as well admit it.'

'I did not and I am not admitting anything.' Her tears gave way to anger and stubbornness. She was not going to be brow-beaten by the police. Her one dread was that they would lock her up in a small cell. She had heard so many stories about that sort of thing.

They left her in a small room off the charge office and for a wild moment she wondered if she could escape, but then she realized that there was nowhere she could go without being found again and if she did run away it would be a sure sign of her guilt. She wondered how Irene had reacted when she was told about the theft.

'I hope she doesn't believe that I did it,' Malele thought. 'I liked her and I wish that I could do lovely things like that.'

It was late afternoon when she was told to go and not to leave Lusaka. Malele walked back to the gallery and found Petson still there.

'I was going to the police station to find you,' he said. 'What happened? We were all wondering and waiting to hear.' 'No doubt Sylvia was hoping that I would be locked up and charged,' Malele said bitterly. 'They tried to make me say that I was a thief, but I wouldn't, so in the end, I was told to go and not to leave Lusaka. Oh Petson, this has been a dreadful day and I am so tired and frightened.'

She felt his arm go round her as he held her tightly. 'I know, I know. I wish that there was something I could do. You know that I believe you. You wouldn't steal like that. I know that. You must go to your house and try to rest. Leah says that she has food for you. Anyone who is harassed by the police is a martyr according to her! Come, we will go to her now. You have had a long day.'

She was grateful to him for believing in her and to Leah for thinking of her. 'People are kind sometimes,' Malele said. 'You and Leah make things better.'

It was during the meal eaten outside Amos and Leah's house that Leah said suddenly, 'You know I think I saw Sylvia pass by your room last night.

It was late and I was coming back from the shower when I saw someone in the darkness coming back towards the main house from somewhere round the back where your room is. I am almost sure that it was Sylvia. I didn't think anything of it until now, and even so it probably means nothing. She may have been looking for the guard or checking the back gates.'

'Did you tell the police?' Malele asked eagerly.

'Bah. Tell the police? No, I did not. I never tell them anything.'

'Perhaps you should,' Amos put in. ' Who knows it might mean something and help Malele. But I can't think how. Sylvia has every right to go there and you aren't even sure that it was Sylvia. It could have been a guest wandering about, they do sometimes and one or two do use the back gate.'

'Leah, please at least tell them. I don't think it will help, but it might. I have never seen Sylvia near my place.'

'I am not sure that it was her so how can I tell the police.' Leah was starting to regret having said anything. 'If I feel really sure then I will, but for now I am not at all sure and I am sorry I said anything. As you say, Amos, it could have been anyone. I do think it was a woman, though.'

Nothing could change Leah's mind about the police and Malele gave up trying as she felt it was a forlorn hope that it had anything to do with the theft.

She went to her room and could not sleep, the worries of the day crowding in on her. She wondered what would happen now. The police would question her again, that was likely. The gallery owner might decide that he didn't want her any more. Sylvia was no longer any sort of friend. Thank goodness for Petson. She could rely on him. It was all too much and when she did fall asleep through sheer exhaustion, she dreamed of being locked in a small crowded cell and not being able to get out again.

Chapter 11

Malele decided that she might as well go to work early the next morning. She was dreading seeing Sylvia and Mr Chona as she felt that they suspected her of the theft and no longer trusted her. Petson greeted her cheerfully and asked how she was.

'Hope that you have stopped worrying. Things will turn out all right, girl from the sticks. Now how about coffee. I need some.'

'What have you been doing that makes you so thirsty?'

'You may well ask. I went out last night with a friend and of course we met two girls and as long as the cash held out we had a party. Now I am broke and thirsty.'

Malele felt a twinge of jealousy. Petson was so often out with girls. He made no secret of it and had no desire to settle down, but sometimes she wished that he felt more attracted to her. Not that she was in love with him at all, but it was hardly flattering to be treated like a younger sister. Then she laughed at herself. The last thing she wanted was for Petson to get serious about her. She had a career ahead and wanted no serious affairs. 'I hope the girl was worth it,' she said tartly.

'Here, take your coffee.'

'Thanks. No she wasn't worth it and in the end she went off with some other guy who was at the bar. Women! not even grateful.'

'Why should we be? What's so great about casual men like you?'

'Now, don't be like that, girl from the sticks. Think of what you would miss without us men.' He grinned and swallowed down his coffee.

'I wonder what will happen today?' Malele asked thoughtfully. Petson had cheered her up, but there was still the rest of the day to get through and Mr Chona and Sylvia.

'The police will give up as they have nothing concrete to go on. That is the first thing, then Mr Chona will claim on the Insurance and that will ease any strain on his pocket, and the whole matter will fade out. Irene Selassie is leaving soon so she will not have too much time to worry us, and she will be paid out.'

'I hope so. Leah has a story about seeing a woman she thought was Sylvia near my room late last night. When I asked her to tell the police, she began saying that it was very dark and she couldn't see properly. Do you think it could have been Sylvia and if so, why was she there?'

'Leah is always full of stories so I wouldn't take it too seriously, but there is no reason why Sylvia shouldn't be in that area. There is the back gate and she could have been checking it, she may have seen a visitor off. A few do use the back gate as they live nearby and it is easier, all sorts of reasons. Ask her if it will make you happier. Although I would love to implicate Angelo, I don't think he was there or one of us would have seen him. There is nothing to go on as far as Sylvia is concerned. Not unless she is in it with him and we could never prove that on the little we know.'

'You were the one who said that Sylvia mentioned me as the thief. How could she? That makes me wonder about her. I did try to like her but now I don't.'

'I shouldn't have told you but I felt that it was best that you knew. No use thinking people are your friends when they aren't. Anyhow she didn't accuse you, just wondered. Forget it. We both need our jobs and unless we can come up with absolute evidence we are stupid to make waves. No one can accuse you of this and the sooner we forget it the better. And don't tell Sylvia what I heard please.'

'I can't forget,' Malele sounded stubborn. 'It is all right for you, you aren't under suspicion. I am. Even though the police have nothing. All I can hope is that they will find the thief, but

97

they aren't likely to waste too much time on this case.'

Later that morning Sylvia called Malele in. 'What happened with the police yesterday? You weren't back when I knocked off.'

'They let me go because they couldn't prove anything. I told the truth that I didn't take the things. I don't know anything about the theft.'

'Well, someone did. There have been too many things going lately. I lost some money a while ago and I don't know who took it.'

Malele lost her temper unwisely. 'No, and I heard your brother saying what about me having taken it. I was in the hall and heard you talking. That time you stuck up for me and I think you thought that he had taken the money. Now you think I did. Well I didn't. And were you outside near my room late on the night of the exhibition? Someone saw a woman they thought was you. If it was you, why were you there?'

Sylvia looked surprised for a moment. 'Who told you that?'

'Someone. It doesn't matter who. Were you there?'

'It is none of your business where I was, but if you must know I saw someone off through the back gate. Does that answer your query?'

Malele didn't answer and gave her a hard look.

'It is sheer impertinence on your part even asking. If I were in your shoes I would be very careful about what I said and did. There is no one else who had some of the jewellery on their doorstep.'

'I didn't put it there.'

'No? Well it is up to the police what happens next, so off you go back to work and let's have no more impudence from you. Put that energy into hard work and you will do better.'

Malele left with all the dignity that she could muster and returned to the kitchen where she went on with her chores.

Every time she heard someone come in through the front door she was sure that it was the police coming to take her for questioning again.

She heard no more from the police in the next week and Sylvia coolly ignored her. Malele felt unhappy and insecure. As Petson said, she did need the job badly and besides she liked it.

Eunice and Boniface discussed it endlessly when she visited them on the Sunday, both encouragingly sympathetic towards her and Boniface angry at the police for even thinking her guilty.

'How dare they? The earring wasn't even in your room. Anyone could have dropped it. I expect the thief went out of the back gate and it fell there and he didn't notice.'

'That's the trouble about being poor and needing a job,' Eunice said. 'One loses the option to walk out angrily if one really wants to stay. And there are so few jobs about.'

'I do want to stay,' Malele said. 'I like the work and I am ... maybe was ... part of the team that hung pictures and set up exhibitions when I was not in the kitchen or cleaning ...   I would never find that sort of job again. I know that, so I am just going on working and hope that I didn't upset Sylvia too much when I lost my temper.'

'Tempers should be controlled,' Eunice said gently. 'But I know how you felt.

I would probably have done the same.'

A month after the exhibition, just when Malele was thinking that things had settled down again, Sylvia handed her a letter with a smirk.

'This is for you from Mr Chona.'

She left Malele to open the envelope. Inside, the typed letter terminated her employment and told her to collect three months salary in lieu of notice. No reason was given other than that the gallery no longer had any need of her services. She had worked there for nearly two years.

Cold with shock, Malele waited for Petson, then handed him the letter to read without saying anything.

'Hell,' he exploded. 'This smacks of Sylvia. She waits a while then arranges for you to go. Nothing said about the theft, but I bet this is what it is all about. The gallery does need you and you are part of it.'

'I was,' said Malele sadly. 'They can sack me like this. So long as they pay the notice there is nothing that I can do. I could go to Mr Chona but it won't get me anywhere so I will have to leave. The letter tells me to be out of the room tomorrow.'

'I wish that I could do something.'

'Please don't try. At least you have a job so keep it. Don't do anything silly.'

'I will miss you,' he said. 'I will miss the coffee and the talk and the help with the pictures. Oh, Malele, it seems so unfair and it makes me wonder if Sylvia is frightened of something. Why bother to sack you when even the police have decided that you have no case to answer.'

'Don't think like that. Keep your job. Promise me that you will be sensible. I would hate you to get into any trouble because of me.'

He nodded thoughtfully. 'You are right. Stop worrying. What are you going to do now? That is the next thing.'

'I will go to Eunice and Boniface again. Eunice said that I would be welcome, and I can help her with the food until something turns up. I can work on my grade twelve and perhaps when I pass that I will find something good.'

'Perhaps.' He paused and sat thinking. 'Take the crayons with you, Malele. I saw the things that you have done and one day you will be good enough to sell on the street. Perhaps even to show paintings, but that will be in a long time. I will collect up paper for you to take and I will keep in touch with you when I can.'

'Thanks. Yes, do keep in touch ... when the girlfriends can spare you,' she added laughing. 'The crayons will go with me and I will try to use them. I don't know if I will ever be any good but I will try.' Then she began to cry and he patted her shoulder comfortingly until she stopped sobbing and went to the cloakroom to splash cold water on her face.

Malele left the next morning. She did not see Mr Chona as he was away at a conference and she did not bother to say goodbye to Sylvia. Petson saw her off, carrying her meagre possessions over to where Boniface worked and where she sat under a tree waiting until it was time for him to go home. The three month's salary was safely tucked into her chitenge cloth. She and Boniface took the bus back to the township and Eunice had left them an evening meal as she was going to be late home. Malele looked round the shabby house and remembered the first time she had come there with Eunice from the bus station.

'It is like coming home,' she said to Boniface. 'You are my family now and I wish that I had come back in a better way. Still I have some money and Eunice can have most of it for my keep.'

'We don't need anything. Not now. You will find another job soon enough and then we can talk about it. I take my second exams soon and, with luck, I will be promoted and the pay will be better.'

'And one day I will pay you back all the money you have paid out for my grades. I haven't forgotten.'

'That is not for paying back. I told you that. Two grades in one year is great, and now the last one. Malele, I am so proud of you and so is ambuya. You are her daughter now.'

'And are you my brother?'

Even as she said it, Malele wished that she hadn't. Boniface was so precious to her, but she did not want to start any sort of affair with him for she knew how sensitive he was about his handicap and how he would never willingly fall in love, but that if he did, it would be totally and devastatingly. She was not ready for that, and not with Boniface.

'For now, but one day it may be different.' Malele had to strain to hear the last words and rapidly changed the subject. It had been so much easier with Petson when nothing was serious for him or for her and his girlfriends were mostly a joke.

Eunice and Malele went each day to sell food at their stand at the bus station.

'I can do with a helping hand,' the old woman said, and for as long as her money lasted, Malele decided to go with her. Eunice was growing old and carrying the pots and the food tired her.

'A young pair of arms is what I need,' Eunice said, grunting as she put down the pot that she was carrying. 'It is good to have someone to help.'

There were slack times and busy times, but generally business was fairly good as Eunice was well-known for her good cooking and reasonable prices. Malele found that sitting about without much to do became boring. She was used to activity and one day she brought along her pencil and sketchbook that Petson had given her and during a slack time she amused herself drawing the people around her. At first a crowd collected to peer over her shoulder, but the novelty of an artist soon wore off and before long she was part of the scenery and was left in peace. Occasionally some youth would pass and glance at her work and make some crack about it, and Malele enjoyed the repartee.

'Hey, is that meant to be people?'

'If you think so. It is up to you.'

'Very funny people.'

As the weeks went by, her drawing improved and she was almost satisfied with the figures that she was sketching. They had lost their stiffness and sometimes she felt that they were recognizable. Boniface and Eunice were full of praise for her efforts.

'And I can't draw at all,' Eunice exclaimed. 'I don't know how you do it.'

'Nor can I, not even a straight line,' Boniface joked. 'Come on Malele, try a proper picture ... you know, colour and all that.'

'Not at work, that is too difficult, but if I can learn about people and how they are, then one day I will do a market scene or perhaps the bus station, but that will be at home where people won't see if I make a mess.'

'You won't make a mess. Have a try.'

'One day I will. I want to be better before I waste the crayons and the paper.'

Malele kept on with her sketching, filling the book with her drawings then spending a few precious kwacha on another plain pad. She and Eunice had agreed that in return for Malele helping, she would have free board and accommodation, but Malele wanted to give Eunice money.

'Certainly not. You are a big help to me and that is worth more than a bed in the corner and some food. When you are a famous artist then you can give me money, or one day when you have a good job. For now give me your labour. That is the best thing.'

There was nothing more Malele could say and the three months salary in lieu of notice was getting smaller as she had to spend some small amounts on herself and sometimes she bought oil or sugar as an extra for the house. Many people passed through the bus station and one day as she was serving food, her old school friend, Shamba came past with two other girls in their school uniforms.

'Hello Shamba.'

Malele was glad to see her. Any familiar face was a welcome sight. Shamba looked startled and for a moment Malele thought that she wasn't going to return the greeting, then she said, 'Oh, hi, Malele. What on earth are you doing here?'

'As you can see, selling food. Where are you off to?'
'School project. We have lots of them. Aren't you at school any more? I am surprised to see you like this. You always had such big dreams.'

'I still have, but I have to live, so here I am.'

'Poor you.' She gave a small smile and turned away.

The girls wandered off, laughing and chattering, and Malele could feel tears pricking at her eyes. How she wished that she too could be with them, smart in a school uniform and careless of the rest of the world.

One slack day as Malele sketched under the Jacaranda trees that were shedding their purple flowers into a deep violet shadow under the branches, Malele was conscious of someone behind her. She turned her head and looked up into a dark face. He was standing in the shade, leaning forward to get a better glimpse of what she was doing and as he met her eyes, his white smile broke across his narrow face.

'He is an old man,' she thought. 'There is grey in his hair and lines under his eyes.'

'Sorry, but I had to see what a beautiful girl like you was so busy with. That's not bad, you know. Talent there all right.'

'Thank you. I keep trying.'

'And succeeding.' He sat down beside her, his long legs folded under him.

'Here, let me show you. If you alter that line a little and stop outlining so much you will have a better effect.' He took the pad from her and began to sketch. Malele watched, not knowing whether to be annoyed at his intrusion or grateful for his help. The help won when she saw what he meant.

He handed the pad back to her. 'There. See what I mean. A little thing, but the difference between the professional touch and the amateur.'

'Yes, it is better, but who asked you to take over?' Malele put the sketchbook down.

He grinned cheerfully. 'No one at all, but in the fellowship of artists when I see how someone can be improved with so little extra knowledge I do help ... especially when the artist is a beautiful girl.'

Malele was suddenly conscious of her dusty feet in their flipflop sandals and her old chitenge. She had so few clothes that she wore the oldest ones to go to work. The man was attractive with his curved aquiline nose and the darkness of his skin. The elaborately embroidered shirt gave him an exotic look and a thick gold chain curved round his neck. But he was old. She recognized that he was an expatriate for his looks were decidedly not Zambian.

'Where are you from?' she asked.

'Nigeria originally, but I was trained as an artist in London and now I teach at one of the colleges here. My name is Kano Okacha.'

'An expatriate?'

'You could say that. Now tell me your name and how you come to be here.'

Malele found herself telling him about herself, cautiously skating over some of the parts, but her story expanding as she sensed his interest. She left out stealing her ambuya's money and the suspicion that she had been under at the gallery. She wanted him to have the best impression of her.

'I work with ambuya over there,' she said pointing to where Eunice was serving out some nshima and relish.

'She is now my mother and I live with her.'

'That is good,' he said. 'Now I have to go as I have a lecture to give, but I will see you again and next time I will ask permission to help you with your art and not blunder in.'

'I am glad that you did. It has helped me a lot.'

Malele watched him walk away, tall and thin in his casual clothes and she hoped that he would be back. 'Only because I want to learn more,' she assured herself, 'he must be at least forty and that is another generation.'

Chapter 12

She fell in love almost unwillingly. All her life Malele had dismissed the idea of being involved with a man as something in the far future, after her career. But as the weeks passed she found herself waiting for him, looking up from her sketching to scan the road in the hope that the tall figure would be coming, for he always walked.

'My daily walk is necessary to me,' he said. 'I have a car, but the body needs exercise and as the college is close by I walk when I have the time between lectures.'

'Then I should see you every day?'

'There are other roads and I vary my route.' It was as though he was teasing her with his absence.

'Absence makes the heart grow fonder they say,' he joked when she said that he had been missing for four days.

'Maybe, but too much makes one forget the person,' Malele retorted. 'Not that that would matter of course.'

'It would matter to me,' he said smiling. She clung to the thought.

'Don't tell me you are hankering after that Nigerian?' Eunice asked. 'I know these foreigners. All they want is to get a girl into their bed and then they try another girl. He is far too old for you anyway, and he probably has a wife and children here or back in Nigeria. There are plenty of decent Zambian boys about, and I thought that you were set on a career and not love.'

'I am not hankering after him and he can have as many wives and children as he likes for all I care,' Malele said defiantly. 'He knows a lot about art and he helps me. That is all. I know that he is old.' She half believed it.

'Well, I am glad to hear it. For a moment I wondered.'

Dressing each morning to go to the station, Malele made

sure that she was looking as neat and attractive as possible. She wished that she had a better and more varied wardrobe and that she could afford hair extensions. He might come that day and she wanted to look her best.

'You must come and see my work in my studio,' he said one day. 'It is always good to see another artist's work and to learn from it.'

'Am I an artist?' Malele asked.

'Soon you will be, and even now I am proud of you.'

'When can I see your work?'

'I will fetch you in the car as I live in Roma and that is a long way.'

'Yes, but when?' She was anxious to settle the date.

'Shall we say on Saturday. I don't work then. I will be here at eleven hours and we can have lunch in the studio if you like.'

Malele nodded, wondering how she was going to tell Eunice that she would not be there to help her with the lunchtime rush. Saturday lunch was not the busiest time, but there were sure to be plenty of customers.

'I will have to ask ambuya,' she said. 'I usually help her then. But there will be no problem.'

'That is up to you, my dear. I will pass by and if you are waiting we will go.

Until Saturday then.'

Eunice said very little when Malele told her that she had been invited out. In a way she was pleased that the girl was beginning to go out more. Until now she had been too self-contained, and the Nigerian was in a respectable job and he was an artist who helped Malele. Her prejudices were unreasonable, but she was worried about Malele. She was too vulnerable, despite all that had happened to her in her short life.

'I can manage perfectly well, my child, but be careful with him. Too many men want only one thing.'

'I know, ambuya, but he is not like that. He is an old man and that is what I ran away from, remember. I need to see other artist's work and he has helped me so much. Please don't worry. I am a big girl now and can look after myself. Not that I will need to. He is only trying to help me.

'All men are like that, old or young.' Eunice was cynical. 'Some are better than others, but that is part of being a man - unless there is something wrong.'

On Saturday he arrived in his Toyota Corolla, Malele was waiting for him and climbed into the front seat as he drew up. She had been ready since early morning.

'It will help me to be an artist,' she told Eunice. 'Okay, I like him, but he is not important.'

'Since when has being an artist been so important?' Eunice asked dryly. 'I thought that you wanted to be a secretary. Art is all very fine, but there is no money in it unless you are very good.'

'I might be very good. You know how hard I have worked at my sketches. He says that I have talent and so did Petson, so I might as well learn what I can. Anyway, ambuya, I am only going to look so what's the fuss?'

Malele felt a sense of excitement at going to his studio which was in a block of flats. They climbed the stairs and he opened the door for her to go in. The sitting-room led into the dining alcove where he had set up his easel. There was the smell of turpentine and there were paintings stacked against the walls. A big studio easel stood in the centre of it. On the easel was a large canvas of a brilliantly coloured abstract painting. Malele stared at it and gradually the bands of colour began to make sense, or at least to give her a sense of excitement.

'That's the latest one,' he said standing beside her. 'I have called it Transition.'

'It is very good,' Malele said shyly. 'The colours are

beautiful even though I don't really know why.'

'That is the beauty of abstract painting. It means what the viewer wants it to mean and if you enjoy it you can make up your own dreams.'

'I heard someone say that you should only paint abstracts with knowledge, not as an excuse because you can't do anything else.'

'True, but I have the knowledge and I can actually draw and do realistic things. This is a development of that, not an excuse.'

'It is the colour that I like so much. One day maybe I will know enough to use beautiful colours like that. One day I want to paint people in markets and at the bus station ... all the things that I see about me all the time. That is what I really want ... if I am ever good enough.'

'You will be. I will help you to be. You are young and there is so much for you to learn, but if you will come to me each Saturday I will teach you.'

'Why?' Malele wondered what his answer would be.
'Why? For various reasons. You have talent and need help. I can give that help and I want to make you into an artist, and also because we are friends.'

'We have only met on the street under the jacaranda trees.'

'Isn't that enough? Malele, I am old enough to be your father; a pity, but there it is, and there is so much you can learn from me.'

'I know.' She was vaguely disappointed in his answer. 'I will come and I will learn. I have only crayons and some paper. Is that enough?'

'For the moment. Then I will let you have some of my old paints and you can learn other techniques.'

He showed her his other paintings and talked to her about them, explaining about colour and colour contrasts and all the other things that made up his work. She listened and sometimes argued with him, but it was only a token assertion of herself. She was swept up in art and the theory of art and in what he said. The time flew by. They ate sparingly from some pizza that he had bought, and drank Fanta out of the bottle, then he drove her back to the bus station.

'Thank you,' she said as she got out of the car. The evening light caught the grey in his hair, but she was unconcerned with age. Kano was no particular age to her. 'I will catch the bus and be there on Saturday morning. I have had a wonderful time.'

'Good. Then we will start work on Saturday. Remember what I have said today and next week we will do so much more.' He drove off, waving to Eunice who looked up from her brazier and gave him a baleful stare.

'And what did the great artist do all day?' she enquired as Malele greeted her.

'Did he bother to teach you or was that only an excuse for the company of a young girl?'

'Ambuya, how nasty you are. I can assure you that he only showed me paintings and talked about them. I have learned so much and next weekend I will go there again and start working.'

'I don't like it at all. Why should he bother with you unless he wants to sleep with you?'

'Because he thinks I can learn to be a good artist and he enjoys teaching.'

'I should have thought that he has enough of that during the week without teaching at the weekends.'

'Ambuya, he wants to teach me. Isn't that enough? One day I will earn money with my paintings and that will be because he has helped me.'

'I still don't like it, but you are not my daughter so there is nothing that I can do.'

'Stop worrying, ambuya, there is nothing more in this than him teaching me.'

110

'I am sure that he can teach you lots of things. He is old enough. Just see that it is only painting that you learn from him. I don't trust him. I shouldn't say too much about this to Boniface if I were you. He won't like it either, and he is fond of you.'

'I know. And I am fond of him. This is learning and that is all. There is nothing wrong in it.'

'Girls are fools so often.'

'I have sense, ambuya.'

'I would like to think so.'

The weeks went by and Malele worked hard, learning how to use oil paint and how to compose a picture. Kano talked about colour, about composition and above all made her see her work in a new light. He opened up a different world to her, but he was a hard taskmaster and some of his criticisms were harsh and reduced Malele to tears. Sometimes she was tempted to throw the work away and to storm out, but something kept her there.

'Shadows on the red earth aren't black,' he said to her when he found her painting black shadows under the trees. 'Shadows take on the colour of whatever they fall upon. Look again when you sit under the trees sketching. An artist must learn to observe. You only think shadows are black.'

She thought about painting for most of her waking hours and when she saw people in the bus station or a tree in flower, she tried to think how she would paint it and what colours she would use. She also thought of Kano. He was in her thoughts too, and she longed to talk of him, but she knew that Eunice would not listen and would have hard things to say about him. Although Boniface said very little, she could sense that he disapproved of her increasing involvement with Kano.

'I suppose that you are off to Roma again today?' he said one Saturday morning. 'How long is this going on for? It was all right for a few lessons but now it is week after week. Has the man nothing else to do?'

'But Boniface, I am learning so much. Look at the work that I am doing now.

Hasn't it improved?' she asked, trying to reassure him. 'I am lucky to have someone interested in teaching me. The college only take people with O levels and I haven't got any.'
'Your paintings are beautiful, but then I always thought them good. I know nothing about art as you know. Don't get involved with him, Malele. He is an old man and you know nothing about him.'

'Of course I won't. He isn't even interested in me that way, and I have a career to follow.'

'And you don't do much about the grade twelve work now,' Boniface said bitterly. 'Once you stayed up late to work on it and now you waste your time drawing. You can draw all day except when you are helping amai, so why do you go on with it at night? Once, all you wanted was to get grade twelve and then become a secretary or something like that. Now you want to be an artist.'

'I have to do a lot. I have started art late and I have to catch up.'

Malele knew really that it was to impress Kano with her industry. He would examine all she had done during the week at each Saturday morning session and comment on how hard she was working. The praise made her determined to keep up the effort.

'If only all my other students worked as hard,' he said and the praise sent shivers through her.

'I am not in love,' she told herself firmly. 'I like him and I am learning from him.' She found herself imagining the feel of his hands on hers and on her body. He remained aloof, sometimes giving her the hope that he was interested in her as a woman; but when she analyzed what had made her hope that he was, she realized that the remarks could have been perfectly innocent and it was only her imagination that read things into them.

The rain was pouring down when she had finished her painting of a marketplace and was waiting for him to come and comment on it. He was working at his easel as he usually did while she painted. The light was pale and the windows were blotted with drops of rain running down the glass. Outside, everything was grey and damp, the puddles forming on the grass and the leaves hanging limply on the branches. She watched him work, a dark figure against the grey light, his palette knife scraping against the canvas with a soft grating sound.

'Finished?' he turned and smiled at her.

'I think so. You had better see and tell me.'

He put down the knife and the palette and came over to her. She could smell the faint perfume of aftershave. He stood silently and she could hear her heart beating loudly. There was tension in the room. Outside, the rain hit the windows in a flurry of sound. She willed him to praise her work and she was conscious of his closeness.

'Well done. I don't think you need to do any more on that. Any more will probably spoil it. It lacks what I call passion, but that will come with time and you are young. When you know more of life you will understand.'

He put his hand on her shoulder. Malele lifted her hand to his and felt a wild surge of longing. He was looking down at her and she shivered as his hand moved against her neck. They stared at one another, then he kissed her gently.

'I am proud of you. You are a credit to my teaching.'

She was in his arms, all restraint gone as they clung to one another, his hands roving over her breasts as she pressed against him. There was no thought in Malele's mind except to be near him. The painting was forgotten. It was the first time that she had really experienced sheer physical desire and the fierceness of it swept over her. She forgot all Eunice's warnings and all her ambitions and for that moment she was wholly his. He buried his face in her hair.

'No, Malele. Are you sure that you want this? I am an old man and you are so young and fresh? This should not be happening.'

'But it is, Kano, and I want it to happen. I love you. I have never said that before to anyone and I have never let anyone sleep with me.'

'Let me teach you about love, Malele. It is a beautiful thing and if you are sure, then let me show you how beautiful it can be.'

'You are my first man,' Malele whispered. 'I will need to be shown.'

He drove her back to the bus station that afternoon and left her there. 'Eunice will know what I have done,' Malele thought in panic. 'I must look different. I feel different and I love him. I don't care what she thinks.'

The afternoon had changed her from a young inexperienced girl into a woman who acknowledged that she was in love. It was a heady feeling.

There were several people waiting for food when Malele reached Eunice and she was grateful for this. Eunice nodded at her and went on attending to her customers. Malele busied herself helping with the nshima.

'Sorry I was late,' she said. 'The bus didn't come so Kano had to drive me back as it was getting late.' The old woman looked at her for a moment and Malele dropped her eyes pretending to be measuring out the relish.

'These buses are unreliable.' Eunice said nothing more but Malele was sure that she knew.

Chapter 13

'I am going to live with Kano,' Malele announced defiantly as she packed up her few belongings. 'I am sorry to leave you and Boniface, ambuya, but I must go. You see ambuya, if you know where I have gone there will be no need to worry about me and I will come back to see you often. Kano says that it would be for the best and then I can paint all day and maybe I'll have a picture in an exhibition. That would be a beginning.' She spoke quickly, half-ashamed at leaving the old woman and the crippled man who had been so good to her. It was not that she was ungrateful, but it was time to go.

'You are making a mistake Malele. We love you as family and now you are going to live with an old man. What happens when he decides to leave and go back to his country? Will he take you? He won't. Wait and see and then where will you be? His is a different world, my child. He is well-educated and travelled and he is amusing himself with you because you are beautiful and because old men like to have a young woman on their arm.'

'No, ambuya. It is not like that. Kano is only forty-five and he will look after me.'

'He will marry you I suppose?'

'Ambuya, I love him and that is what matters. Through him I will be an artist who sells paintings and I will learn about his world. Is that so bad? Here, I am a nothing, fighting to pass grade twelve. I am grateful to Boniface for helping me and to you both for letting me share your home. All this means is that I will go into a different world, but I will still be part of yours and I still love you.'

'There are many forms of love. What you are doing might be called lust if one were cruel.'

'Try to like him, ambuya. You would if only you could forget your prejudices.'

'A girl of eighteen hardly knows her own mind. Still there is nothing that I can do to stop you. It is Boniface that I mind about. Boniface has never felt strongly about a girl before and although he hides it, I know what he feels. Have you bothered to think of that?'

'Yes, and I hate leaving him. I love him like a brother, ambuya, and he knows that. There is nothing else. It is Kano that I love and must be with.'

'So be it. I hope that we'll feel able to pick up the pieces when you need us.

At the moment I am too disappointed in you to think that far ahead. Malele, how could you? Think what your mother and your grandmother would say.'

'They are in the past. I had to leave them and now I must move on again. I love you and Boniface and I am not going far away. I will be back to see you, I promise that.'

Eunice shrugged. 'Go and I wish you well. Try to be kind to Boniface when you say goodbye.'

Malele moved in with Kano that afternoon, hanging her clothes in the big wardrobe that was full of his. He watched her doing it, holding her round her waist and kissing her neck.

'I was afraid that you wouldn't come. I nearly came for you but you had said not to. Was it very hard to leave?'

'Yes, and I felt bad about it, especially about Boniface who has had so much go wrong in his life. He was getting too fond of me and I only love him as a brother.'

'And me? I am no brother?'

'No brother at all, only the man I love and the man I am with.'

They were in the flat together, loving and excited by each other. Kano worked all day at the college and Malele cleaned and cooked and when the chores were done she painted; at the small easel that he had given her beside his big one. He would see what she had done during the day and before the evening meal would talk about what she had done and make comments

116

on it. His praise took her into a heady state of euphoria and his criticism dragged her down, but always he encouraged her to try harder and they ended in lovemaking.

Sometimes she was lonely, waiting for him to come home, and she formed a tenuous friendship with a neighbour. Nancy lived in the flat next door and when they met on the stairs, the two women exchanged greetings. Then they began to visit one another, calling round at any time during the day. Nancy was small and plump, but smartly dressed, and Malele admired her sense of style. She was the wife of a doctor who worked at one of the private clinics and had made an effort to be friendly with Malele, sensing the girl's insecurity with her new and smarter life. Her twin children were at school in the morning and she had the time to visit Malele. Sometimes Malele wished that she wouldn't come when she was painting, but she enjoyed having her company.

'One day I will be as smartly dressed as you are,' Malele said to Nancy as they chatted together. 'I have never had enough money to be able to be smart.'

'Nor had I at first. It is something one learns when the time comes. You look good in your chitenge and in what you have. If I was as slim as you are I would be very happy.' Nancy pinched the fat round her hips ruefully. 'Katele likes fat women, so he assures me, but that apart, I would love to be slim. Childbearing, especially of twins does nothing for one's shape. Not that I was ever slim. Short yes, but with plenty of meat on my bones.'

'I have never thought about it really. I have always been thin and in the village, I was just one of many thin girls who envied the ones with big bosoms. Before that I was a young schoolgirl determined to have a career. Then my father died and we went back to the village.' This was as far as she got telling Nancy about her past life. It was something that she wanted to forget.

'Humans are never satisfied are they?'

117

It was a week later that Kano came home and handed Malele an envelope.

'Here is money for you to get yourself some new clothes,' Kano said as he handed her the money. 'What you have is not really suitable for the social life we will be leading. I want to take you out to hotels and to parties and you will need clothes for that. And get your hair styled. You said that you wanted to have extensions so go ahead and get them. You will be beautiful.'

'I thought you told me that I was already beautiful,' Malele teased.

'You are, and without clothes you are more beautiful still, but I want you to be part of my circle when you meet my friends. It'll be better for you that way. Women hate to be dressed less well than their acquaintances. Go with your friend Nancy and ask her to show you how to shop and what to shop for. She is a smart woman and will know what to buy and where to buy it.'

'It seems such a lot. Can you really spare it?'
'Remember, I am an expatriate here and I get an expatriate salary.'

'How much do you get? Is it a great deal?'

'To you, it would seem so. In terms of the real world, not so much. Anyway,

take this and leave me to worry about the finance. I imagine you have nothing yourself?'

'Nothing. I gave the last of what I had to ambuya. She wouldn't take it so I put it under her bed mat where she will find it. She made me take a bus fare with me in case I wanted to leave you.' Malele laughed at the memory.

'And do you?'
' No, and I never will. This is forever and one day you will be proud of me as an artist.'

The next day she went across the landing to Nancy. 'Of

118

course I will come with you,' Nancy said. 'There is nothing I like better than shopping, especially when I am spending someone else's money. Your husband will be pleased when he sees what you look like once we have gone to town.'

'Nancy, he is not my husband, at least not yet. I love him and I am living with him. Does that bother you?' Malele was terrified that Nancy would mind.

'Why should I care? I didn't really think that he was married to you. You come from a different background. I know that. Good for you girl, going up in the world. I was only a trainee nurse when Katele married me, and my father was a guard at someone's house. There are so many of us coming from humble homes and climbing upwards, but in some circles it is best to pretend to be married and say nothing about your family.'

Malele listened and learned from Nancy. Together they went shopping, buying Malele designer label clothes that came in the huge bales of salaula clothes that were sent over from the States and sold in the teeming salaula markets very cheaply. The clothes were donated by Americans who had become tired of them, and Malele found everything from lacy bras to smart dresses there.

'These things are beautiful,' she said to Nancy and pictured herself parading them in front of Kano. He would love the black lace underwear and she shivered with pleasure at the thought.

They spent three hours at a hairdresser and when she was shown the back of herself in the hand-held mirror, Malele was amazed at how sophisticated the long ponytail of extensions made her look. It was exactly what she had dreamed of when she had first seen Sylvia.

'Wow,' said Nancy. 'This has really changed you into a woman. Before that you could have passed as a schoolgirl. Just wait until Kano sees you. He will be even crazier about you than he is now.'

They took the bus back to Roma, travelling as far as the Catholic Cathedral and then walking the short way to the flat. Malele clutched the plastic bags that contained her purchases. 'Give one to me,' Nancy ordered. 'You must be sick of carrying them.'

'No, I want to carry them. I have never had so much before and I want to experience every moment of them.'

Nancy laughed. 'Tell me that in a year's time. One soon gets used to having things, but I understand how you feel. I spent the whole of my first salary on clothes and my father was furious with me. He said that I had no money sense. After that I came down to earth and became more sensible. When I married Katele he was working at the UTH as a houseman and we were very poor even though he had done all those years at the university. I had to go on working, but as a married woman I could not go on training to be a nurse, so I got a job as a receptionist in a clinic for not bad pay, then when Katele got the job with the private clinic he wanted me to stop. I got pregnant and that was that. We manage on his salary.'

'One day I will sell paintings,' Malele said. 'I used not to believe that but now I do. Kano has taught me so much.'

Kano was late home that night and Malele waited impatiently for him to come. She showered, then put on the briefest of lace panties and a low-cut wisp of a lace bra, topping them with a strappy print dress that made her feel daring and half-naked as she was unused to having her shoulders so bare. Then she placed all the other purchases on the chair to show him. She painted her lips with the silvery lipstick that Nancy had lent her and dusted her eyelids with a pearly eyeshadow that Nancy had insisted would make her look even more stunning. Malele stared at herself in the mirror and hardly recognised the face in it. The long ponytail and the braided hair transformed her into another being and the eyeshadow accentuated her dark eyes. Malele fingered the

120

ponytail lovingly. This was something that she had wanted for so long. She smiled at her reflection, her teeth very white against her skin.

'I am almost beautiful,' she said aloud. 'Not exactly as I would want to be, but I am surprised at how good I look. That is what a bit of money and care does and I am lucky that I have it.'

She heard him open the front door and made herself walk slowly to meet him, swaying her hips in a provocative way and laughing at his reaction as she spun round to let him see her hair.

'Heavens, Malele. Is that really you? I thought that some beautiful model had decided to make her home here. This is wonderful. You are lovelier than ever.'

'Come and see the things I have bought.' She led him into the bedroom and showed him the shoes and the clothes. 'I spent all the money.' For a moment she was anxious.

'That is what it was for and I am amazed at how much you have.'

'Salaula. These things are almost brand new and Nancy says some have designer labels. Just imagine anyone not wanting the clothes and sending them here.'

'They did not look beautiful in them.'

'Do I?' She wanted to hear him say it again and again.

'Like a finished painting. Very beautiful.' He stood back and let his eyes rove over her. 'Your hands and feet still bear the marks of life in the township and walking in your flipflops, but that will change and you will be perfect.' His words were like a slap in the face to Malele.

'My hands and feet?'

'Yes. They are not perfect yet, but they will be.'

'And does that matter so much to you? I thought that you loved me for what I am and not because you want me to be perfect.'

'I love you, but to me everything should be as perfect as it can be. It must reach its full potential ... like your painting. You want that too and this is also what I want for you.'

'I see.' The pleasure in the evening had dimmed.

'And if I never fully please you?'

'You will.'

'But if I don't?' she persisted. 'Will you love me less?'

'You were potentially beautiful when I first saw you under the jacaranda, and now you have come so much further. That is what matters.'

'But do you love me?' She had to know.

'I love all beautiful things and you especially because you are the one with me.' He took off her clothes slowly and lovingly and stood looking at her as he would have at a carving. Malele trembled as he watched her. 'Am I good enough?' Anger was taking the place of disappointment. 'I am as I am, and you took me as I was. All this talk of perfection! What the hell is wrong with you, Kano. Am I some piece of art that you are buying?' Her voice was growing shrill and she hoped that Nancy would not hear it but she could not stop.

He took her in his arms. 'You are as you are, and that is what I want. Now be quiet or Nancy and Katele will wonder what is happening and come over. We have better things to do than to talk to them.'

After Kano had left the next morning Malele hung all the new clothes up and thought about the night. She took a long look at her hands and feet and had to agree that they were less than well-kept and callous free, but what did it matter? The remarks that Kano had made still stung and unsettled her. Did he only want perfection? If so, it was unlikely that she would ever really please him, but she would try to improve her hands and feet. The thought of perfectly groomed nails, painted some exotic silvery colour appealed to her and she determined to try to achieve them, partly for Kano and partly for her own pleasure.

It had been so less complicated with Eunice and when she was alone, but Malele recognised this as the price of upgrading her social status.

'This is what I want,' she thought. 'And Kano loves me.'

Chapter 14

'We are going to the Embassy cocktail party tonight,' Kano reminded Malele as he went out of the door on his way to work. 'I am looking forward to showing you off so get yourself geared up for it.'

Malele nodded. She was nervous about the cocktail party. This would be the first one that she had accompanied him to and she realized that he expected her to do him credit. She went over to see Nancy who was busy doing the house.

'Nancy, we are going to the Embassy cocktail party this evening. Have you been to this sort of thing before? I have only been to gallery openings and that is not the same. I don't want to let Kano down. You know how he is.'

'Oh, these cocktail parties are all alike, probably the same as the gallery one.

All you do is to go in and then stand around making small talk with all sorts of people, some you know and some you don't. When the speeches are over you hang around for a bit and then go home. It's nothing to them and usually quite boring. Make Kano take you out to dinner after that. You will be all dressed up anyway and the Pamodzi is on your way back and the food there is good. Not that we ever go, but that is what I have heard.'

'I wish that I wasn't going.'

'Rubbish. You will enjoy it when you get there and it will be a new experience for you. There is so much that you will have to learn now that you are with Kano. I had the same problem. My goodness, the knives and forks used to scare me silly whenever I went to dinner. There were so many of them. And at my home, before I was nursing, we only went in for the traditional eating and didn't use knives and forks.'

'Kano likes the Western way of eating. It would be so much easier to use my hands and dip the nshima in the relish but he insists on us having formal meals. He cooks brilliantly and so I don't have to do much cooking.'

'More fool him, but one gets used to it. Anyway all the cocktail food is finger food as a rule. As far as the knives and forks go, just start at the outside of the setting and work inwards. That is usually safe enough and watch what other people use.'

'Dear Nancy,' Malele thought. 'She always has so much common sense. She makes things seem easy. I wonder if she knows how Kano expects me to be so perfect. I would never tell her. That is something between him and me, but I find it more and more worrying. Why should I be so perfect when I don't expect him to be? That is the price of loving someone so much.'

She was determined to learn the new way of life but sometimes she thought wistfully of a simpler way. She knew that she would find it hard to go back to life in a poor township. Even in the three months that she had been with Kano, she found that in her visits to see Eunice and Boniface, she had become critical of their comparative squalor, of the cold water and the outside taps and the communal lavatories. It was a way of life that she hoped she had left forever.

'That's my girl,' Kano said with approval as she waited for him to collect the car keys. 'Perfect, even down to the nails.' Malele laughed with pleasure. 'If you only knew the effort I put into the nails. Oil paint is not the easiest thing to get out of one's hands.' She looked down at her silvered nails. 'They will get longer, but this is practical.'

He kissed her. 'It is worth all the effort, my perfect one. Why not reach your full potential? And you have. Even your paintings are full of passion now, and you are a fully-fledged

125

woman ... and a lovely one. If I was a rich man, I would load you with diamonds and precious stones.'

'I don't want diamonds, my love. You are all I want ... you and my painting. I never even imagined that I would ever paint and now it is part of my life.'

'Part of our lives. Yours and mine. We both paint and we both love, so we have all we need.' He held her tightly for a moment. 'And now to our first reception together.'

The reception had begun when they reached the door of the embassy and they joined the queue to greet the ambassador and his wife. Malele noticed that she was in a traditional costume and had made no attempt to compete with a modern dress. Most of the other women were smart in their cocktail dresses and Malele was glad that she had opted for a simple black dress with a low-cut neckline.

'I am still not used to showing so much,' she had said to Nancy. 'I'm still a conventional Zambian villager at heart but I am learning!'

'With a body like yours, make the most of the modern fashions. Forget about how it was in the village and when you were a maid. This is on another social level altogether.'

The room was full of the sound of people talking and laughing, the wafts of expensive scent and the warmth of the crowd swept over Malele and she felt shy and awkward; but after Kano had introduced her to several people and she had seen the admiration in the men's eyes, she relaxed and began to enjoy herself. Kano was so obviously proud of her.

Malele noticed several people that she recognised from the gallery openings and in the distance she saw Petson talking within a group. She had not seen him since leaving the gallery and, as Kano was busy with some of his friends she pushed her way over to Petson. He was just moving off from the group to get another drink.

'Hi, Petson,' she smiled at him, watching his stunned surprise as he recognised who she was. A look of admiration came over his face.

'Girl from the sticks!' he exclaimed. 'For a moment I didn't even know you and I wondered who this stunning bird was and how I could have forgotten her. You look fantastic, Malele. Come and tell me all that has happened to you. I can see that it is good. I wondered where you had got to and I always meant to ask Boniface, but he had moved to another place.'

'Yes, he went to a better job when he passed his exams. I should have come to see you but I hated the thought of the gallery.'

'It is still the same. Sylvia, Mr Chona and the couple at the back. We're still having exhibitions and there's another assistant to help me so we must be doing well. Now, let me get a drink for both of us and then into a corner to hear all about things.'

She asked for a Fanta and it grew warm in her hands, the glass beading with moisture as she talked.

'So you live with him now?'

'Yes.' She sounded defensive. 'It is because I love him and he is a great artist.'

'No need to explain, girl from the sticks. These things happen and you have done well obviously. The thing I am interested in is your painting. I know Kano's work and we have had it in the gallery sometimes ... not one of our bestsellers with the general public, but the ones that know about art pay big prices for it. One day I will see yours. Where do you live?'

She gave him the address and wondered if he would come to see her. She had few visitors at the flat and so far none of her old acquaintances. Eunice said that she and Boniface were too busy and Amos and Leah did not know where she was. Anyway they would not have felt at ease in the smart flat. She sighed. Life could be complicated.

'Why the sigh?'

'No reason. I am very happy where I am now, but there were good times in the past.'

'Live for the present is my motto. If things are going well don't look back.

From kitchen maid to what you are now is quite something and I am pleased for you. If I had known how gorgeous you were going to be I might have taken you out myself.'

'You were far too busy chasing other girls!'

'Sure, but we were good friends.'

'We still are.'

The time passed quickly and Malele could see Kano looking for her. 'That's my escort,' she said indicating him. 'I had better go.'

As she moved away she almost collided with a woman who was wearing a long purple sheath and, as she apologised for her clumsiness, Malele saw that the woman had the exhibition necklace around her neck. For a moment she stood staring at it, and her first instinct was to snatch it and shout out that it was a stolen thing and that she had been under suspicion because of it. Then she recovered her senses and simply smiled. She turned to find Petson and pulled him aside from the man he was talking to.

'That woman in purple has the stolen necklace,' she said quietly. 'Who is she?'

'No idea,' he replied. 'Where is she?' Malele pointed her out. 'Don't let her see you looking,' she urged, 'but she is just behind you near the door.'

Petson waited a moment, then casually glanced round the room, hardly pausing when he saw the woman, but he had a good look at the necklace. 'It certainly looks like the one we lost. Let me go closer and chat her up and see who she is. Come with me.'

'I can't. Kano is waiting for me, but Petson, what are we going to do?'

'You must come with me and make certain that it is actually the necklace. You knew it and so did I to a lesser extent. If it is, nod your head at me and I will find out who she is and where she lives. Then I will go and tell my friend at the police post and he can go on from there.'

They went across to the woman who had joined her friends. They made for a gap in the circle and Malele smiled at her again and nodded vaguely around the group as though she knew at least some of them. Petson pretended to recognise the woman in the purple dress. He moved closer to her.

'I know we have met somewhere before,' he said, using his charm. 'I should remember where it was, but I can't.'

'I don't remember you either,' said the woman firmly. She was obviously used to this type of approach, but at this sort of party one could never be sure that one hadn't met before. 'One meets so many people at this sort of thing that it is impossible to remember them all.'

'Ah! but I never forget a face,' Petson went on. 'Especially a pretty one.'

Malele wanted to giggle at his blatant flattery, but instead she nodded her head at Petson. The necklace was the stolen one without doubt. Its pattern was so distinctive. He saw her and went on talking to the woman. Kano was hovering on the outskirts of the group, obviously waiting for her, and she knew how he hated to be kept waiting. It was one of their bones of contention.

'Petson, I have to go, but keep in touch and find that address won't you?'

It was the best she could do and she hoped that Petson would be able to do something about the necklace. She had no desire to become embroiled with the police. Once was enough, and even though this time it would be different, Kano would not like his friends to think that he had befriended a suspected thief; her version of her past had glossed over that, and also the taking of the money from her grandmother. There were some things best left out of her history, especially now.

'That man you were with looked familiar,' Kano said as they walked to the car.

'I am sure that I have seen him somewhere before?'

'Probably at the gallery. He was there when I was.'

'Ah, yes. That's where. I bet he was surprised to see you here and looking so wonderful. I must say that all my friends thought you a knockout and envied me. That is what is so good about a special possession ... other people wish they had it and applaud your good taste.'

'I am not your possession. I live with you but you don't own me.'

'Sorry, a slip of the tongue. No, I don't own you, but in a way you are my creation.'

'I hate it when you talk like that. Yes, you have helped me become what I am, but so have others and remember that.'

He opened the car for her. 'Come on, Malele. Why all the fuss. You were a star tonight and that has made me proud of you. You are so young that people wonder what you see in an old man like me and that makes them wonder about me too. That is the way the world goes round! Enjoy it.'

'I do, but I want you to love me for myself, not as some pleasing thing that you own. Is that why you took me to your home? Because I looked good and because I could paint a little?' She was annoyed at herself for raising the subject. The evening had been so good and now she was on the verge of a quarrel.

'If you had been different I would not have taken you. That is the chemistry between us. If I had been a street vendor would you have wanted me? No, you would not, so you see how we suited each other's needs. Don't question everything.'

He made love to her that night. She lay against him afterwards, content and dreaming of her future with him. Let him have his funny little ways. He had done so much for her and she loved him.

Nancy had a telephone, so the next day Malele waited until Kano had gone to work and phoned the gallery. She knew that personal calls were not encouraged and she hoped that Petson would answer the telephone in the hallway. Sylvia had her own line and that went through to Mr Chona. She dialled the number and waited impatiently as it rang. On the third ring Petson picked it up.

'Art Gallery.'

'Petson, it's me. What happened? Did you find out and did you go to the police?'

'Yes, madam. And may I have your phone number so I can let you know?' Malele knew that Sylvia must be with him and that he was unable to discuss things, but at least he had done something. She gave him Nancy's number. 'This is a friend's number but you can leave a message and I can ring you.'

'Fine. Thank you, madam. I will let you know.'

Malele could imagine Sylvia asking who it was and what she wanted. No doubt Petson would make something up, but she wished that he could have told her more.

He rang late one afternoon and Nancy came running over to call her. 'Telephone for you, Malele. I bet it is that gallery friend. Let's hope that he has done all he should.' Malele picked up the receiver. 'Petson?'

'Hi, girl from the sticks. Are you looking beautiful today?'

131

'What has happened? ' She cut the pleasantries short, anxious to catch up on events.

'All done and I get a blow by blow report from my police pal. They went to her house and there was the necklace in her drawer. Seems that she didn't know it was stolen and at the time she was having an affair with Angelo. Or rather he was trying to woo her, hence the present. She hasn't got the rest of the stuff so he must have sold it for funds. The police have picked up Angelo, but Sylvia is implicated as Angelo says that she took the things and gave them to him.'

'So Leah was right. Sylvia was round by the back gate and handing the jewellery to Angelo.'

'That's what it seems like. I expect he pressured her so much that she agreed.

He had plenty of money from her and this was another way of getting funds.'

'And blaming me,' Malele said bitterly. 'I am so glad that I saw the woman. Now what happens?'

'I have formally identified the necklace and so has Miss Selassie. That is the first thing and the police have had a statement from Angelo and one from Sylvia. She is suspended from her job and there is not much doubt that she will be convicted by the court when the case comes up. Angelo is only the receiver of stolen goods so he may get off lightly. It is a pity, as Sylvia was pushed into stealing I am sure. She is less to blame than Angelo in a way.'

It was good news, although Malele felt a sneaking sympathy for Sylvia and anger that Angelo should get off lightly. 'So now they know I didn't take anything?'

'Sure, and Miss Selassie is upset that they ever blamed you and so is Mr Chona. If you want the job back I am sure it could be arranged.' She heard the teasing in his voice. 'Not a hope. I have spent hours getting my hands into good shape and that would put them back to what they were!' Malele joked.

'Seriously, no. I hope that I never work as a maid again. It was a beginning and I enjoyed it, but now I have other things to do.' She was full of triumph now that she had been proved innocent. The suspicion had hurt her.

'You certainly have. One day I want to see your paintings. Perhaps the gallery will take them?'

'Perhaps. Kano says they are now worth exhibiting, but still need to grow, whatever that means. It would be nice, and it could happen. Kano will tell me what to do when the time comes.'

'I will visit you one day when you invite me. Then I will see them. In the meantime keep in touch. I will let you know what happens in the court.'

Chapter 15

'Nancy, I think I am pregnant,' Malele said as the friends sat together in Nancy's flat. 'I have missed twice and that must be the reason.'

'That's wonderful,' Nancy exclaimed. 'I am so pleased for you. Children are such a blessing. All the hard work of looking after them is more than worthwhile. Get it confirmed and then tell Kano if he doesn't know already. He will be so proud of you.'

'Yes, I think he will.' Malele let doubt creep into her voice. 'I hope he will. I hope that he won't be annoyed with me. We hadn't planned to have children, at least not yet, and they do disrupt one's life. Kano likes his peace and quiet and I am not sure that I will be a good mother.'

'Rubbish.' Nancy put her arm round Malele. 'Most women feel a bit uncertain at first. I certainly did, and when I was told that it was twins I had moments of panic. But that passed and now I am so glad that I did have twins. Kano will be delighted and so very caring.'

'I hope so. But what happens when I am bulging and clumsy? Kano wants me to be such a credit to him and he wants me to be smart and well-dressed.'

'He will be proud, you wait and see. You can still be smart and the fact that he is to be a father will make him doubly proud. Will you get married now?'

'I honestly don't know, Nancy. I would marry him tomorrow but Kano says that being tied would destroy what we have now. So long as I am with him it doesn't really matter does it? There are so many single parents with partners these days.'

'That sounds like Kano talking! Yes, there are, and it is none of my business at all. I am happy for you if you really are pregnant.'

With her pregnancy confirmed, Malele waited for a suitable opportunity to tell Kano. She was determined to choose her moment carefully, and it was after supper, when he was relaxing in his chair, that the moment came.

'Kano, you are going to be a father,' Malele watched his expression as she said it. He looked startled.

'But I thought that you were the one who agreed to take precautions. We agreed on that and now you tell me this.'

'I was, but something must have gone wrong.' Malele willed him to stop scowling. 'I am sorry, these things do happen.'

'So it seems. And now?'

'And now? Well, it will be born in six months time, and we will be parents.

Kano, dear, just think, there will be a son or a daughter for you and we will be a family.'

'I am not sure that my plans include a family. I told you that when you came to live here. We are two artists and there is true passion between us. You know that and I know that. We are two creative people and our work is what we create. That is our life.'

'We seem to have created something else,' Malele said ruefully. 'That is a fact of life and it is not going to change.'

'No, but our lives will. And what time will you have for painting with a baby screaming round the place? Our work is part of our love and now you are spoiling it.'

'I can do both Kano.' She stroked his hair. 'A baby won't upset things, and as you said, experience shows in one's painting and this will add to mine and to yours.'

'I doubt it. Nights without sleep and a pile of nappies drying in the kitchen. I have seen this before.'

'Before? What do you mean? Kano, have you other children?' The thought hit Malele and shock made her less cautious.

'Are you married? Is that why you won't discuss marrying me? Every time I mention it you pass it off and tell me that it would spoil things. Is that why?'

'The past has nothing to do with you. I have told you that. We are together and that is the present.'

'I love you, Kano, and I can't bear it when you close up on me. I know that the past is your business, but now it is mine too. This will be our baby and it should have a mother and a father.'

'It has, and a piece of paper with our names on it won't make things any different, my conventional little girl.' He paused. Malele could hear the faint music from the television. She clenched her hands nervously. This was not how she had planned the evening to be. Kano sat up. 'Okay. So you are to be a mother and I am to be a father. It is not something that I planned and not something that I would have chosen, but perhaps a man needs the world to see that he is capable of creation. Perhaps having a young life to mould and to guide is a good thing. Who knows, with both parents as artists he may become a greater artist than either of us, and with us to show him and to teach him, it should be possible.'

'It could be a girl? Would you mind?'

'A boy, it will be a boy.' Kano was definite.

'Of course. But it is so far away that we needn't worry about it at all. We will be proud of him or her, whichever it is, and we will be happy together.'

He was fierce and passionate that night, loving her with a kind of desperation as though things would not last and he wanted to make the most of their time together.

'My beautiful one, If you had not told me that you are pregnant I would not have known. You are as slim and lovely as ever.'

But Malele was conscious of the changes in her body and brooded on the child, imagining what it would look like and how she would care for it. She was no longer afraid, a deep maternal feeling had replaced the earlier apprehension, and as she worked, she sang the village songs to the unborn child.

'He will be called Aquilla,' Kano said. 'It means "the worker", and he will be famous and I will have helped create his fame.'

'If it is a girl I will call her Mia,' Malele thought and did not say anything aloud. Kano was so determined that the baby was to be a boy. 'Mia means mine and she will be mine.'

Eunice and Boniface had received the news when she had gone to visit them.

'Eh, and now you will marry him I suppose?' Eunice asked. 'There are too many single parents about these days and a child needs a father.'

'It has a father,' Malele said. 'Whether we marry or not it has a father who will care for it.'

'And he will not marry you even now?'

'It is better this way. And what does a piece of paper matter between people who love each other? Would you prefer him to buy me with a bride price of goats and cattle? I could have had this once and I ran away. No, ambuya, I am willing to have things this way and we are so happy together. Kano was shocked at first, but now he is full of pride.'

'So long as you are happy,' Boniface said. 'That is the important thing. I wasn't pleased when you went to Kano. That I must confess, but if you are content then so be it. It will be a beautiful child if it is like you, and you are looking so well and happy that I can only be pleased for you. Do you still do your lessons or is that a thing of the past?'

'I will go on with them one day, Boniface, but for now I paint and that is more important. Getting grade twelve was the big thing in my life and I am so grateful to you for helping me get there, but now my art comes first.'

'And the painting? Will you sell the paintings one day?

They looked good to me before you took up with Kano, and now I haven't seen anything you have done for a long time, but I am sure it is even better. You need to get a market for them, then the grade twelve will not matter as a stepping stone to better things. You will have your art and your career.' She heard the bitterness in his voice. 'Then you won't need anyone to help you and if Kano leaves you, you will be able to manage.'

'Kano won't leave me. Why should he? Boniface, please understand that we are in love.'

'Perhaps. Anyway what do I know of love. That is something for others. It must be a two-sided thing and for me that is hard to find.'

Malele was touched by guilt that she could not feel love for him. Not that kind of love. 'You will find love, Boniface. One day.'

'No. A girlfriend perhaps when I am earning big money and exams are a thing of the past, but that is all; and I will understand that and not be lured into thinking that what they pretend is love.' He laughed harshly. 'There is no fool like an old fool and I do not intend to be an old fool.'

'I love you like a brother, Boniface, and when the child is born I want it to know and love you as an uncle or an elder brother. Ambuya, you will be a grandmother to it and you will be its family.'

'And your own mother? Does she not deserve to be told about this child?

Love makes one selfish, Malele. That is a fact and once the child is born you must write to your mother and let bygones be bygones. A child needs relatives. That is part of our culture and it is a good one. Don't try to go against it just because you have a rich partner and a career of your own.'

'Ambuya, so far I have no career of my own, but maybe it will come, and Kano seems rich because you are poor, but he is not really rich. When Boniface has all his exams over with he will be well paid and your life will change like mine has. We are rich enough, but not too rich and you will be the same.'

'So Boniface tells me. But what will an old woman like me do with a different lifestyle?'

'Enjoy it. There is so much to be said for having light and hot water and not having to scrimp and save all the time. It is an easier life but with its own problems too.'

'There are always problems. Still we shall see.'

'Ambuya will accept it when the time comes,' said Boniface. 'We could move into a better place now, but she wants to stay with her friends in the township. When I pass the last exams then we will find a better place and her life will be less hard, but I know that she will grumble and pine for the old ways that she has always known. She will at first, then she will be content and will understand the benefits.'

'That's my son! It is probably true and I am almost ready to move, but this is where all my friends are and what I have known for so many years. Life does change and I thank God for a son who will care for me in my old age. I hope that yours will do the same, Malele, for I doubt if Kano will.'

The weeks passed and Malele longed for the baby to be born. Her ankles swelled and she felt clumsy and ugly, but Kano was full of pride at becoming a father and made plans for the child. He was convinced that it would be a boy and the closer the birth date came, the more he spoke only of a boy. He would have only the best that they could afford and he would go to the top schools. Malele sighed and hoped that if the child was a girl he would not be too disappointed.

'Nonsense,' Nancy said. 'All men think they want a son, and then when a girl arrives they dote on her and can't imagine why they ever thought of a boy.'

Petson had contacted Malele and invited her to exhibit in a women's exhibition that the gallery was to hold. He had been to the flat to see the paintings and had approved of the work that Malele was doing.

'Girl from the sticks, how much you have learned. These might even sell with a bit of luck. Your Kano must be a good teacher to get you to this standard so fast.'

'It would be more polite to say that it was my talent,' said Malele. 'But you are right. He is a good teacher and I do work hard.'

'You always did. Remember that correspondence course that you sweated over every evening? That was hard work. I know that you are a worker. I am in charge of selecting work and if you bring three paintings to the gallery in two weeks time I am sure that Mr Chona will give them his blessing and they will go in the exhibition. There is no Sylvia now to upset you and I will make you a cup of coffee myself as a mark of my respect.'

He was the old teasing Petson and she was delighted to think of her work hanging in the familiar gallery.

'It is a beginning,' Kano agreed when she told him what Petson had said.

'I am pleased that the young man liked the work. Just so long as he admires and doesn't touch.'

'What do you mean?' Malele asked.

'Don't let any young men cast their eyes at you, my lovely. Otherwise they will have this old lion to reckon with.'

Malele began to laugh. 'Are you jealous? It was a heady feeling. 'In my present condition I would doubt if any young man would be interested, and in any case Petson is a great ladies man and has no intention of being serious with anyone. He would run a mile if he thought that any woman was seriously considering him as a husband. He is strictly a roving lover.'

'I am glad to hear it. Youth is always attractive and hard to compete with.'

'There is no competition, Kano my dear. I love you.'

On the night of the opening of the Women's Exhibition, Malele and Kano drove to the gallery and went into the well-lit hallway. Mr Chona was there to greet them, welcoming Malele as though there had never been any shadow on their relationship. For her part, Malele thought of the contrast between her wretched departure with Sylvia seeing her off the premises and the present greeting.

'I never imagined that I would be welcoming you as an exhibitor,' Mr Chona said as he shook her hand. 'I like your work and I hope that this is the beginning of a long association with the gallery.'

'I hope so too.' Malele said coolly. 'Servant to exhibitor. It surprises me also.'

It was unkind to remind him, but she felt that she had earned this small revenge. She heard Kano chuckle beside her. She waved at Petson and took a catalogue from the desk as she passed. It was strange seeing her name in print along with all the other names and she went with Kano to see where her paintings were hung. Petson had placed them in a well-lit area and Malele felt a shock of pleasure at seeing them there, glowing in the spotlights. Then self-doubt crept in and she wondered if they were as good as all the other works there and every fault became glaringly apparent.

'They are fine,' said Kano reassuringly. 'Some of the best here.'

She smiled gratefully. 'I was beginning to wonder. Thanks.'

The gallery assistant whom she did not know came bustling up and placed a red star under one of Malele's paintings.

'You have sold one already,' Petson exclaimed as he came up. 'Well done, girl from the sticks. Now come round and meet some of the other artists. Come along both of you.'

141

Malele smiled and nodded and shook hands as she went round, too excited to be self-conscious and she admired the other artists work.   Kano was greeting old acquaintances and introducing them to Malele.

'My pupil,' he explained proudly. 'This is her first exhibition and she has already sold one.'

She smiled inwardly. Kano was always happy when he had some part in another's success. He was less keen when he had nothing to do with it. 'This is the beginning of the career that I have always dreamed of,' she thought. 'Exhibiting and actually selling, even though it was not for a lot of money, and the baby to come, and Kano beside me being proud of me. The girl from the sticks is on her way.'

The baby was born at the hospital. It was an easy birth and Malele was surprised that things had happened with so little drama. She was drowsy from the drugs she had been given and heard the midwife say, 'A boy.' A great sense of thankfulness swept over her. Kano would be satisfied and she did not mind. Either was fine. The baby screamed loudly and she reached out to hold it. It was then that she saw that the child had a deformed arm. It was twisted and the hand had only two fingers and no thumb.

Chapter 16

Kano came to see his child soon after he was born. Malele had wrapped him in a shawl which concealed his withered arm. She handed the baby to him wordlessly and as he took the child into his arms, Kano was smiling and filled with pride.

'He is as beautiful as you are, my dear.'

'Yes, he is beautiful.' She did not know what to say about the arm. Perhaps, if Kano loved him, he would not mind. She watched as Kano unwrapped the shawl. His face changed and he stood staring at the child who began to whimper.

'He is a cripple. My son is a cripple.' He thrust the screaming child into Malele's arms.

'This is no son of mine. This poor deformed thing will never be whole and I will not accept him.'

'Kano, he is beautiful apart from the arm and that is not his fault. He will grow up nearly normal and his other arm is perfect. Please Kano, don't reject him. He is bright and strong and it is only the arm that is wrong. He is your son and my son and we are responsible for him.'

'I am not responsible for a cripple. There are no cripples in my family so the fault must lie with your family. He is yours but not mine and I do not wish to see him.' He walked out of the ward leaving Malele to comfort the child and to hug him to her as she wept.

'He will come round to loving Aquilla,' Nancy said when she saw the baby.

'It is his pride that is hurt. He was so determined that he would have a perfect son that this is a shock. Still, the child will grow up and be a useful person. There are so many worse things than this, and he is a beautiful baby. Mine were not as beautiful, I have to admit that.'

'He is a fine child,' Katele said. 'One day there may be

143

something a surgeon can do with the arm, but even if there is nothing to do, Aquilla will compensate for the arm and live like all the other children.' He patted her arm. 'He will grow to love the child as Nancy says.'

'I wonder. Everything has to be perfect in his eyes, and now he has fathered something less than perfect. For myself, I love him and it makes no difference, but Kano is different.'

'Kano needs to grow up,' Katele said fiercely. 'He is behaving like a spoilt child and thinking of no one but himself. If he could see some of the sad things that I see in the maternity wards he would think himself lucky that this is no worse.'

Katele and Nancy stayed for the visiting hour, but Malele kept expecting Kano to return and say that he was sorry and that everything was all right. Nancy shared her anxiety.

'I am sure that Kano will be back to see you, Malele. But if you need me you know the number to ring. Congratulations on a fine son. He will give you so much pleasure.'

Kano did not come to the hospital again and when she and the child were due to leave, she had to call a taxi to take them to the flat. It was less bother than calling Nancy. This was something between Kano and herself. She was thankful that he had paid most of the clinic fees in advance. Kano had gone to work when they arrived and Malele had to borrow money for the taxi from Nancy.

'You should have phoned,' Nancy scolded her. 'I didn't ask Kano if he was going to collect you as he has hardly been here. He only comes in late at night and I don't see him, I only hear the door slam.'

'It is lucky that I have a spare key in my bag, otherwise I wouldn't be able to get in.'

Malele opened the door. The familiar smell of turpentine and paint wafted round her and she thought of how naive she had been the first time that she came to the flat. So much had happened since. There was a big finished painting on his easel and once again she was struck by the power and the colour of his work. He must have put in hours of work over the past two days, probably working late into the night as he sometimes did.

'I have food prepared for lunch,' Nancy said. 'Put your things away and come over. We can catch up on all that has happened in the last few days and there will be plenty of time to get things ready for Kano when he returns.'

'I am not looking forward to that. Oh Nancy, this should have been such a happy occasion with Kano being with me and carrying Aquilla up the stairs. Everything should have been so wonderful and now look at us. Kano away and Aquilla and I all alone.'

'He is a selfish brute, that is all I can say. Katele is right when he says that he needs to grow up.'

'He has done so much for me.'

'Only because it suited him. I am sorry, Malele, he is behaving badly and you must know that. What sort of a man rejects his own child?'

'Kano is not like other people. He is an artist who wants things to be perfect.'

'Oh, come off it Malele. The hard fact is that he is a spoilt child and it is no use sticking up for him, even if you do love him. You, too, need to see things as they are. Remember that I will do all I can to help you, but I am furious with Kano.'

He returned late that night, drunk. Malele was waiting to greet him. She had dressed with care and made herself as attractive as she could, hoping that she would please him. He glared at her.

'Don't wake the baby,' she said as he slammed the door.

'We took a taxi back as you weren't there.'

'I had no intention of being there. I told you that.'

'So you did. Sorry. Have you had anything to eat?' Malele was determined not to quarrel, not on her first night back.

'I am surprised that you had time to make a meal. I have eaten and I don't want anything. Yes, open a beer for me. I might as well have that.'

The baby started to cry. Kano reacted angrily. 'Shut it up, I can't stand that noise. Get the beer and then shut it up. For a cripple, it has a good pair of lungs and a loud voice. A good shaking would soon put an end to all that.'

Malele did as she was told. He was in an ugly mood and for the first time she was afraid, not so much for herself but for the child. He took the beer from her. His face was haggard and she could see the stubble on his cheek where he had missed places with his razor.

'In the morning you can get out and take the child with you. I don't want either of you here when I get back. I am going out to somewhere more peaceful after I have had my drink, and I don't want to see you here again with the child. If you want to farm him out, then maybe I will have you back, but not the child. A cripple is no use to me and I will not have it here. The choice is up to you. It is your fault that he was born and your fault that he is deformed. You are no sort of a mother for a child of mine.'

'You are throwing us out?' Malele was incredulous. 'Are you really throwing us out? What about support for Aquilla and what about me? Do you really think for a moment that I would leave him?'

'You make the choice. You are not legally anything to do with me, only a pupil who came to study and I have achieved what I can with you. I took you from the street and you can go back to the street. I will give you nothing and as far as your painting goes, I will do nothing for that. Who even knows if the child is mine? Can you prove it?'

'How dare you!' Malele's temper flared. 'How dare you suggest that he isn't your child? There are such things as DNA tests now, in case you haven't heard of them. But Aquilla is

146

better off without a monster like you as his father. I will not be here when you get back and I hope that I never have the misfortune to see you again. You are disgusting and so wrapped up in yourself that I must have been blind not to have seen it before.'

'Goodbye, Malele. And don't take anything that is not yours. I warn you about that. The police have long arms and I would not hesitate to send them after you. Your clothes and the baby clothes are yours to take, but that is all. Oh, and the baby. In our tribe, cripples were left to die and that is how it should be. I could do it myself. The rest of the goods belong to me. Even your pictures and paints, for I was the one who paid for the canvas and the rest. I had great hopes for you but they are gone.'

'So will we be gone, you stupid, childish, conceited man. I don't want any of your things.' She tried to slap him across his face but he caught her arms and twisted one behind her back.

'A common little street tart. That is all you are. Now down on your knees and say that you are sorry for what you did.' He gave her arm an upward thrust which caused her to gasp in pain and forced her to her knees. 'Say it.' He twisted again.

'I am sorry,' she was sobbing with pain.

'And you are sorry for inflicting me with a cripple.'

'I am sorry.'

'You had better be. All this effort wasted. All the hours that I have cherished you and bought you clothes. You came with nothing and I made you into a beautiful woman. Now go back to being a prostitute again, at least I have taught you the art of loving. At least you can satisfy the men you will have, thanks to all I have shown you.'

He let her go and she lay on the floor looking up at him. It was unbelievable how he had changed. The smooth facade had gone and he was coarse and drunk and out of control. Malele

147

felt cold with fear. He was so strong that she was afraid that he would really harm her or worse still, Aquilla. There had been something uncontrolled about it and next time he might be worse.

'You are drunk,' she whispered. 'Please go. I will be gone in the morning.'

He slammed the door shut as he left and she heard him clatter down the stairs and then the car drove off. All her rage and misery overwhelmed her and she threw herself onto the bed, stuffing the pillow into her mouth to prevent herself from wailing out loud. She didn't want Nancy and Katele to hear her weeping. She had loved him and now all that was destroyed. She would never trust a man again. The crying of the child forced her to get up and once she had comforted him, she started to pack. Her rage at the way he had behaved made her impervious to hunger or the lateness of the hour. She wanted to scream and cry and the urge to hurt him was like a physical force.

Money was the first problem. Kano had always given her what she needed and apart from the sale of the picture, she had earned nothing in the past year. The picture money she had spent on a pair of designer trousers for Kano.

'I even owe Nancy for the taxi,' she said aloud.

She knew that Kano had kept some cash in a locked drawer in his desk, but as she had never had cause to go there she had no key and no idea how much there was in it. Once, she had inadvertently seen him putting away some dollars that a purchaser had given him for a painting, but otherwise she had almost forgotten about it. She went to the drawer and found it firmly locked. She tugged at the handles but nothing happened. She went through the contents of the rest of the desk and found no money, only receipted bills, old newspaper cuttings of his exhibitions and a letter from some girl who was obviously in love with him, but as there was no date she could not tell if it was old or recent, and to her surprise she found that she didn't care. All that mattered was to get away. And to do that she needed money.

She went into the kitchen and took one of the sharp pointed knives. Gingerly she pushed the point into the keyhole and tried to turn it but soon gave up. In the videos that she had seen, it had always looked so easy when a thief had opened a lock, but the reality was very different. In desperation she began to hack away at the wood, chipping out the lock. The knife broke and clattered to the floor. It was getting very late. She found a big screwdriver and levered the lock away from the drawer. There was a loud crack and she tumbled backwards. The drawer was opened and she hurriedly went through it. The money was stashed in an envelope and with shaking hands she tossed it onto the table and began counting it. Some of the notes were dollar bills, and there was a bundle of Kwacha ten thousand notes in a rubber band. She counted the notes hastily and pushed them back into the envelope which she placed in her handbag, leaving out enough to repay Nancy. The total sum, allowing for converting the dollars, would keep them both for a while if she was careful. The child woke again and cried, so she fed him, soothed by the warm thrusting mouth against her breast. Thank goodness she would have food for Aquilla at least.

Regretfully, she discarded some of the fancier clothes that she had accumulated. There was no space in the small suitcase for them and they would not be needed in the village. The future could look after itself. She finished packing as the dawn light showed faintly in the sky.

Malele had no exact plan for the future, but she knew that she had to get out of Lusaka or Kano would have the police after her for breaking open the drawer and taking the money. Also, she was afraid of what he might do to herself and Aquilla. The most sensible thing would be to go back to the village. She had never specified where it was, so he would be unable to find her. She hoped that her grandmother would welcome her back, and perhaps her mother. It would be only for a time, then she could perhaps return when Kano's contract was over. To go to Eunice would be to court disaster. That was the first place that he would have searched. The thought of the village and her mother frightened her, but it was the safest place. By catching the bus at the bus station she could get away early, before Kano returned, and she could also say goodbye to Eunice if she was there. Sometimes the old woman went to the station to catch the breakfast trade.

As it grew light, she scribbled a note to Nancy telling her that she had been thrown out and was leaving Lusaka, but would be in touch. Then she put the money for the taxi loan in with the letter. She would slip it under Nancy's door as she left. The big painting caught the early light from the window. Very deliberately, Malele took a kitchen knife and slashed the canvas until it hung in tatters. She was panting with the effort, but she was also filled with a glow of satisfaction. That would hurt him more than the money. She slashed another canvass which was against the wall, then flung the knife aside and began to collect up her own things. She packed a few of her own canvases in the suitcase she had taken, pulling them from their stretchers and rolling them up into a tube. There were too many to take, so she left some behind. The paints were too heavy to bother with so she left them, taking only her crayons and her sketchbook. Art would have to wait. His clothes were hanging in neat rows; so, as a parting gesture, she picked up a pair of scissors and cut pieces out of the ones she knew were his favourites. She closed the wardrobe carefully. Let him make the discovery when he wanted to wear something. The thought of his anger made her laugh. Revenge was sweet, whatever people said to the contrary. The main thing now was to leave for the impulsive damage to his clothes and the paintings would also be a complication with the police.

150

She picked up Aquilla and wrapped him in his shawl. The cot would have to remain; a pity as she had chosen it so lovingly and he had looked so sweet lying in it for the brief time she had put him there. The suitcase was heavy and she staggered under the double burden, her arm still aching from Kano's assault. Pausing, she slipped the note under Nancy's door and went on down the stairs.

There was hardly anyone about in the grey dawn and by moving down the road, she was able to catch a roving taxi to take her and the child to the bus station. She hoped that Eunice would be there but she was not, so Malele scribbled a note which she sealed in an envelope and gave to the watchman at the entrance. He would pass it on to Eunice and Boniface. She owed them an explanation and they had not heard of the birth of Aquilla. Tears filled her eyes at the thought of leaving them and her friends. They seemed all the more precious now that she was leaving.

She was at the front of the queue for the Chipata bus and soon she was sitting in the front with Aquilla in her arms and the suitcase stowed on the top of the bus. It was full when the driver announced that they were leaving. As the vehicle swung into the familiar road, Malele could see the jacaranda tree where she had first met Kano. It was no longer flowering and the leaves were yellowing and falling. Eunice's stand was still empty.

When Eunice and Boniface read Malele's note, Malele was long gone.

'It is probably for the best,' said Eunice sadly. 'I loved that girl and was sorry to see her waste herself on that Kano, but now it is best that she goes to the village and stays there for a time. Goodness knows what will happen, but at least she has gone and I doubt if Kano will go to the police over this as he really is in the wrong and he won't want people to know how he has behaved.'

Boniface said little, but there was a deep well of loneliness in him now that Malele was no longer there.

Chapter 17

The bus trip took eight long hours, lurching over the potholed roads and occasionally stopping for the passengers to relieve themselves and to purchase a cold drink or bun at a wayside tavern. Aquilla wailed and complained, then settled down in Malele's arms to sleep for a while. They were squashed in the front of the bus, sharing a seat with an enormously fat woman who said she was a marketeer going back to her village to see her grandchild. She peered at Aquilla and exclaimed at his arm.

'Poor little boy. What a handicap to begin life with, but children are amazingly good at coping with this sort of thing and in time you will hardly notice. And your husband?'

'He rejects the child, so I have no husband. We have left.' Malele stroked the child's head. The woman's words cheered her and echoed what she thought.

'Oh, men! We need them and we love them, but so often they are the weak ones who cannot accept setbacks like this. My own husband is kind, but it is me who does the earning. You are young and pretty and there are many men in the world.'

'I am off men,' Malele said firmly. 'I will make my own way, but for now I will stay in my village.'

The marketeer held Aquilla while Malele went in search of some food at one of the stops and by the time the bus reached Chipata, Malele was sorry to see her go. The incessant chatter had helped to pass the time and a hard life had made her worldly-wise. Her comments on life amused Malele.

There was no one to meet Malele of course. She and Aquilla dismounted from the bus exactly where she had waved down a lift from the lorry on the morning she had run away.

'And here I am back again,' she said to the child. 'Back and with you. I do hope that ambuya is still here. She was very old when I left and I haven't heard anything from the village since then. I love her, Aquilla and you will too. She is so much kinder than amai. Amai will be fierce and disapproving when she sees us, even though deep down she loves me, and if ambuya is there she will smooth things over for us.'

She wished that she had been going back as a great success. It would have been so much easier. Presents, success and something to show for all her time away. Instead she had only Aquilla with his withered arm and no husband. That would count against her as far as her mother went. She sighed and hitched him higher on her back. She was unused to walking far and her feet ached. The path was dusty and the suitcase dragged at her arm. She rested for a moment in the shade and then went on into the village. It was growing dark when she got there and the smoke from the cooking fires was making blue smudges against the sky. Malele went directly to where her ambuya lived. There was no one about that she recognized and she was glad of that. To her town accustomed eyes, the village looked small and shabby. Even the townships in Lusaka were far less primitive. Here the huts were small and many were still in the traditional round shape with walls made of sticks and mud under the thatched roofs. It had not changed much at all since she had last seen it.

'Ambuya,' Malele called as she approached the hut. 'Are you there? It is Malele come back to see you.'

There was no reply. A mourning dove called in the trees and the sound of voices from the neighbouring huts sounded through the dusk. Malele shivered and called again, afraid to make too much noise and attract other people, then she heard the well-remembered voice answering her.

'Malele? Are you back after so long? Wait and I will

154

come out. My sight has gone, but I am still alive and I have waited for this moment.'

The reed mat over the doorway creaked and moved outwards and a small figure came out of the darkness of the hut, bent and shuffling, but unmistakably her grandmother.

Malele hugged her, smelling the old familiar smell of woodsmoke and age.

'Ambuya it is good to see you. I was so afraid that you would not be here.'

'I am not dead yet as you can see. And what is this?' The wrinkled hands felt the child on Malele's back.

'He is my son, ambuya, and the reason that I have returned here.'

'My great grandson. Give him to me and let me hold him. Where is your husband? Or is this some unfathered child?' The voice sharpened and the blind eyes stared past Malele. She took the baby and sat down on the stool, feeling for it with her foot. 'There is much to tell me, mwana, and I have all the time to listen.' She was running her fingers over Aquilla who lay quietly, his dark eyes watching her. 'He is very young, scarcely out of the womb.' The fingers touched the withered arm and felt the hand. 'And his arm is twisted and his hand malformed. What is all this? Why have you come back? There is so much that I want to know. Have you seen your mother?'

'You are the first person that I have seen here. Amai will be angry and difficult and I wanted to come to you before I had to face her.' Malele sat beside the old woman who was whispering to the child, little phrases of love.

'I took your money, ambuya. You know that and I am ashamed of what I did.

I had to go. Now I will repay it for I have some money. That is the first thing.'

'I was glad that it was of use. When you went, I was afraid and wondered if I had done the wrong thing in telling you about it, for I knew that you would probably take it and go. A young girl is so vulnerable in a city, and there was such a hue and cry here when they found you gone.' She smiled. 'I think it was mainly the prospect of losing the bride price as far as your uncle was concerned, but your mother grieved in her own sour way. I said nothing about the money.'

'The money gave me the freedom to go. Was my intended husband angry? He was so dreadful.'

'Furious, and couldn't understand why you didn't want him.' There was laughter in her voice. 'His pride was dented and now he has another poor wife who is nothing but a servant to him ... and a breeding machine who shows the world that he is still a virile old goat.'

'Thank goodness I went.'

'Now, I am listening and I want to hear all that happened. It is better that you stay with me for the night, then go to your mother when it is light. She is well and content and you will find her softened by time ... not that she will ever be a sweet woman, but she is less angry. That is what the village life has done for her. She has not remarried and lives alone while your uncle looks after her.'

They talked for a long time, eating the small meal outside the hut with the child fed and asleep on Malele's back.

'You have had many adventures,' Esnart remarked when Malele finished telling her the story. 'My life here has been so dull compared to your short one, and I remember Eunice so well. God must have intended you to find her and I am thankful that He did. She is a good woman and she has cared for you like a mother. Now it is time to go to sleep and in the morning we will go to find your mother.'

The reunion with amai proved to be less difficult than Malele had feared. After the first shock and the initial stiffness, Malele found herself taken into her mother's home, and Aquilla brought out all the love and caring that amai had in her. The arm was accepted with little comment.

'You have brought something precious into my life,' her mother said. 'Not that I approve at all of you being a single parent, and that lover of yours sounds dreadful. You would have done better to marry the man we chose for you. I thought that your main objection was that he was so old, and look what you took on. Almost as old and a foreigner as well. Didn't even marry you which Alec Zulu would have done, and paid a good bride price too. I suppose that someone will have you now that you have the child, but there will be no bride price to speak of.' Malele smiled. Her mother was not nearly as fierce and complaining as she remembered her and she no longer resented her authority.

'Amai, I have come back here because I needed to, not to find a husband. As far as I am concerned, I have no intention of ever marrying. I have Aquilla and when time has passed, I will go back to Lusaka and see if I can earn a living with my paintings. That is my plan and one day I will do it, but for now I am here. I have some money so I can pay our way. I am not some beggar who wants charity. You are my mother, so I came to you. If you don't want me, we will go and live with ambuya.' She had told Esnart how she had taken the money and the old woman had nodded her approval. 'Serves him right. Stealing is wrong but that is not stealing. It was due to you and the baby.'

Malele had not mentioned slashing the canvases and the clothes. At the time it had pleased her, but later she regretted it a little and decided not to tell anyone. It had been childish and she had no desire to be thought immature.

'No, your place is here. I am Aquilla's ambuya and I will care for him in my home. Your grandmother is far too old to be bothered.'

The reunion with Silas had proved to be more difficult and it was weeks before the tensions between them had died down. Aquilla helped, but even pride in the child made little

157

difference to their relationship at first, and it was not until Alec Zulu made it clear that he no longer harboured any resentment against Malele that Silas relaxed and began to accept her. Zulu was perfectly happy with his present wife and, as the district had appeared to accept his version of what had happened, and that he had chased Malele away, he could afford to be generous.

'I could tell that she was nothing but a whore,' he explained to anyone who would listen, 'and I had a lucky escape. I am better off now.'

The lack of running water and electricity worried Malele at first and she sometimes hated the primitive conditions in the village. There was a well with a pump, but water had to be fetched and there were no hot showers.

'It won't be for ever,' she told herself as she struggled to carry the heavy buckets from the well. 'One day I will just turn on a tap and switch on a light.'

'You have grown soft with town living,' amai grumbled. 'Be glad that there is a well.

Gradually these luxuries began to be less important and she slipped back into the ways of the village. Aquilla was spoiled by both his grandmother and by Esnart and Malele was amused to see how her mother doted on the boy.

'I never remember amai making such a fuss over me,' Malele said as she and Esnart sat together. 'To me she was different.'

'That is a grandmother's privilege, and besides she was unhappy in the town. Age softens one you know, but she was a good mother to you in her way.'

The monotony of life made Malele restless. 'This is all right for now,' she thought, 'but what about the future? I can't stay here forever, much as I love ambuya and amai and my friends. I need to get somewhere, to have a career. All my life I have wanted that, and now it is no different. The only thing is how?' Tears of frustration filled her eyes, then she forced herself out of her self-pity. She would succeed somehow. This was only a step on the way.

The two older women were only too pleased to look after the child when Malele went to visit the school and agreed to take art classes in the afternoon twice a week.

'We have no money to pay you,' her former headmaster explained, 'but if you could come and show the children how to draw and maybe make clay things, it would mean so much to them. I do have some extra paper which a VSO left behind and there is always clay. Paints are too expensive for the school to buy, but we have pencils.'

'It will do,' Malele said.

'We can learn to make charcoal sticks and the children can draw with them. I would like to help, and this is something that I can do. For myself I have a few crayons and they will do for my pictures.'

She worked and taught and in the teaching she remembered the things that Kano had shown her. The children loved her and were willing pupils and she began to enjoy her unpaid teaching, but she wished that she could earn some money for herself and Aquilla.

She began a series of charcoal portraits of Esnart. The stark blackness of the charcoal sticks that she had brought with her were a sympathetic medium for the likenesses and the powerful blind face came to life on the rough paper. She really wanted oil paints but the discipline of the charcoal forced her to adapt to the monochrome tones and their simplicity gave the work added force.

She was running her class one afternoon when the head teacher appeared with a woman who was being driven in a smart Discovery vehicle.

'Malele, this is Miss Selassie from the European Union. She is doing a tour of the province and has come to inspect the school.'

Surprised, Malele recognized the woman who had made the jewellery for the gallery exhibition. She wondered if the woman would recognise her. After all, she had been the kitchen maid who helped arrange the items and she had only been with Miss Selassie for the afternoon. She smiled and waited.

The woman, smartly dressed in a trouser suit, held out her hand. 'But I know you. You helped me put out the exhibition at the gallery in Lusaka. I do remember you, and you were so very helpful to me. What are you doing here? You had left the gallery when I asked about you and then I was transferred for a year.

'I have come home for a while,' Malele said. 'Now I am teaching the children.'

She did not elaborate.

'I heard that you had become an artist. I am sure that someone told me that.

Didn't you exhibit at the Women's Exhibition? I am sorry to be so vague, but I have only recently returned to Zambia and I have lost touch.'

'Yes. I did exhibit, then I came home.'

'There was some sort of scandal at the gallery. Some of my jewellery was stolen and later they found that the secretary had taken it for her brother. That was after I left. I got paid by the insurance so I wasn't too upset, but it was a nasty incident.'

'I know. They thought that I had taken the things,' Malele said. 'They didn't want me any more and for a time that was bad, but it led to better things and they found the real thief.'

She was surprised at herself for saying so much. It was the first time she had spoken so openly. Even to Kano she had glossed over the theft, ashamed that she had even been a suspect. Deep inside herself she began to laugh. Here she was, ashamed to have been a suspect when all the time she had taken money from two people. It was a crazy world. She said nothing and hid her laughter.

'Show me round and tell me what you are doing,' Miss Selassie said. 'And I would like to see what you yourself are doing. The head teacher tells me that you have done some wonderful portraits in charcoal.'

'I try. The problem is that we have nothing here, and no funds to buy things even if the art shops in Lusaka have them.

The children would love paints but we have none, so we make do.'

Later she went with Miss Selassie, driving down the rough track to her village. A crowd gathered round the smart vehicle and the driver chased the small children back from the shining paintwork. Malele took Miss Selassie to Esnart's home where the old woman welcomed her by kneeling and clapping in the traditional way.

'She keeps drawing me,' she said with a laugh. 'I would have thought that there were prettier subjects, but maybe they have other things to do. The drawings are in the hut where Malele keeps them. Go and fetch them, child, and give your friend a chair to sit on. It is a long time since I had a visitor from outside and I wish that I could see you. Let me trace your face with my fingers so that I have an idea of how you look.'

She ran her hands gently over Miss Selassie's face, memorizing the shapes and by the time Malele had collected up her drawings, the two women were talking as though they were old friends. Malele held up the portraits one by one. Some had become smudged as there was no way of fixing the charcoal, but the sheer power of the drawings showed through any imperfections. The months of practice had honed Malele's skill. She drew with an economy of line that captured the essential character of the sitter, old or young. To Malele, every portrait had terrible imperfections which she had not noticed before. She waited silently, her heart thumping with apprehension and excitement.

'They are incredibly good, Malele, especially as you are battling with poor paper and lack of fixative. They are wasted

161

here. Maybe I could arrange an exhibition for you in Lusaka at our headquarters. We have good hanging space there and I think a lot of the diplomats would be interested. The only thing is that you must have better paper and so on if you are to sell, so if I send you some, will you use it and do about twenty portraits that I can show? These black and white drawings are unusual and I would like an exhibition of them.'

Malele felt the joy rising in her. 'Oh, I would love to do that.' Then the thought of Kano rose like a spectre before her.

'It might be difficult for me to go to Lusaka though.'

'Nonsense. When the time comes you can get a bus ticket and bring the pictures with you.'

'There are problems. Maybe I shouldn't go.'

'What problems? It all seems simple to me.'

'There are problems,' Esnart put in, speaking slowly. 'Let me tell Miss Selassie what they are if you are too silly to do so. Malele had a man there, an artist, who gave her a child and who has threatened to kill her if he sees her again. That is the problem.'

'Who is the man? Someone I know?'

'His name is Kano Okacha. He is a well-known artist who lectures at the college. He is a Nigerian and I am afraid of him.' Malele said haltingly. 'The child had a deformed arm and he wanted to kill it.'

'Kano Okacha. Yes I know that name and I have seen some of his work. Very beautiful if hard to understand.' She paused and thought for a moment, then smiled.

'There is nothing to worry about, Malele. He has left and in fact I was at an official party a few weeks ago to say goodbye to him. That is why I remember. He has been transferred to somewhere in West Africa, and he must have consoled himself, for he had a very pretty girl with him, another Nigerian. He didn't say anything about having a bad experience or anything like that, and there was no talk of the police.'

162

'Oh.' Malele sighed with relief and all the joy surged back again. 'Oh, I would love to have an exhibition. Will you really send me paper? I need good charcoal sticks too as mine are nearly finished. I have a little money and I can pay a bit.'

The thought of Kano with the pretty Nigerian did not worry her at all, beyond feeling a fleeting sympathy for the girl.

'I expect the EU can manage a bit of paper and so on out of its cultural funds,'

Miss Selassie said gently. 'And some paint for the school. That is one of the projects we like to sponsor so there will be no problem there. I will arrange to send the things and will write to you regarding the exhibition. Now, may I take one of these drawings as a sample to show my boss. I am sure that he will love it.'

'Please have it as a gift,' Malele said. 'I would like you to have it. The thought of an exhibition is so wonderful and I will count the days before the things arrive.'

Chapter 18

'So there are twenty-five different portraits and sketches for her to choose from,' Malele said as she dusted her hands on a piece of cloth, then sprayed the fixative over the latest charcoal drawing. 'It doesn't seem possible that I have actually done so many. Now I will write to Miss Selassie and say that I have finished. Then she will arrange the exhibition for me.'

'Then you will go and we will wait another three years before you return?' the old woman asked.

'No, this time it will be different. I am not running away like a frightened child. I will take Aquilla with me even though amai wants him to stay here. He is part of me and I want him with me. Now that Kano has gone there is no danger to him. Besides, Eunice and Boniface have never seen him and they are like my family too. When the exhibition is over I will come home.'

'It is strange to hear you use the word home for the village. When you were a child you so much wanted to be in town.'

'It is home now, but there is the town too and I still want to be there. It is like being two people, one content in the town, one in the village, so I should be happy in either. You are my family here and there are my friends and the school and all the things that I have come to treasure. But in the town there are Eunice and Boniface and other friends, and if I am to have any sort of career in art, I must spend time there and meet people who can buy my work and help me to go on.'

'Young people lead a wonderful life now. In my day there was none of this for us village women, but perhaps we were more easily satisfied and lacked ambition.'

'You have done well, ambuya. You grew up in a different age. If you had been young now, goodness knows how much you would have achieved.'

164

'Maybe. But that is mere dreaming. I shall be sorry when you go for I am old and death is waiting for me. That is life. Life then death and we have no say in when things happen.'

'Don't die ambuya, not while I am away.'

Malele said the words lightly, but she knew how much she would miss her grandmother when she died. It was something that she did not wish to think about.

'Who knows, but your coming back with Aquilla and being here has made my life full of happiness that I never expected. Be successful, my child, and keep striving. I am proud of you. So is your mother and indeed the whole village. Even, Zulu, although I suspect he is still annoyed with you for running away, but he knows that you would have been an impossible wife for him. It would never have worked.'

'No.' Malele laughed. 'I still shudder at the idea, but I suppose he is not as bad as I thought him. Not as a husband though. I need to get together with his poor wife and give her some thoughts on gender equality.'

'No, leave her in peace. She knows no better so why upset her when she can do nothing about it?'

'That's a pacifist outlook, ambuya, but in a way I agree. Let her be.'

Most of the village turned out to see Malele off when she went to Lusaka. Amai and Esnart and the rest of the family came with her to the bus stop, one of the young men carrying her case and another the slim wooden box that the village carpenter had made for her drawings. Some of her pupils waved and cheered as she boarded the bus and settled into her seat, Aquilla in her arms. It was so very different from her last hasty departure and her unheralded arrival a year and a half ago.

When the bus reached the station, Malele waited for her case and the drawings to be unloaded. She left them in the charge of one of the guards and went out onto the front steps to see if Eunice was there. She had told no one of the date of her arrival, although Nancy knew the approximate date, so there was no car to meet her. She would take a taxi to Nancy's flat.

As she stood in the old familiar surroundings, she saw Eunice coming down the road, her heavy dishes in her hands. Pushing past people, Malele started to run towards Eunice, calling out her name. The old woman looked up and with a cry of joy hurried towards her.

'I missed you so much,' Eunice said after the first greetings were over and they were sitting round the brazier. 'I got your message when you left and cried for you, but now you are here it is like a miracle. I was afraid that I would never see you again. And this is Aquilla? My, he is a fine child. You must be so proud of him. Come and sit with me and tell me all that has happened. You said that you were staying with your friend, but you know you would have been welcome to stay with me. We have moved to a smart flat because Boniface has passed all his exams and can now afford the rent. He is always telling me to stop work, but somehow if I did, there would be such a gap in my life that I would not know what to do. I may retire after this year as I am getting old, but for now I am happy working. He is away for a week in Livingstone on the firm's business.'

'It is so good to see you again, and my grandmother sends her greetings to you. She is blind now, and frail, but she remembers everything and is as bright as ever. She talked so much about when the two of you were young.'

'We old women love talking. Now I have talked enough and I want to hear all about what you have been doing.'

After a while, Malele said that she had to go or the guard would stop minding her cases and they would be stolen. She looked about for a taxi and waved one down. When her cases had been stowed in the boot, she hugged Eunice again.

'I will be in touch and I have your new address. Greet Boniface for me and make him come to the opening of the exhibition with you. It will be in about two weeks time, but the date isn't settled yet. I will let you know.'

They drove up to the entrance to the flat. There were so many bitter-sweet memories there. Nancy opened the door at the first knock, smiling and welcoming.

'Welcome, stranger, it is so good to see you. And look how big Aquilla is.

The village life must have suited him. And how are you, Malele? You are looking well and as slim as ever, lucky thing.' They hugged each other.

'Thank you for saying that we could stay, Nancy. I have missed you and Katele so much, but now I am here.'

'Why didn't you tell me that you would be here today? I would have brought the car to the bus station and saved you a taxi?'

'I wasn't sure when I was coming, not the exact time. It was the easiest way and I found a taxi easily enough. I also saw Eunice which was wonderful.'

'Now, let me help carry the cases to your room. It is all ready for you and stay as long as you like. We have so much to catch up on. That wretched Kano left about three months ago, so he is out of the way.'

'Was he angry when I went?' Malele didn't like to ask about his reaction to the damage she had done.

'He was furious and came banging on our door to find you. Then when you weren't there he went back to the flat. There was all sorts of coming and going for a time and someone said that you had damaged his paintings, but he never came near us again. He obviously regarded us as your friends and avoided us. Did you damage his paintings?'

'I was angry and I took a knife to some of them and I cut up his clothes, but I am ashamed of what I did. I was so upset and angry that I wasn't thinking straight.'

Malele hung her head. Nancy giggled. 'Well done you.

He needed a lesson from what you told me in your letter. I shouldn't let a little thing like spoiling some of his belongings worry you. I would have done the same I expect.'

'It was inexcusable and childish.' Then Malele began to giggle with Nancy as they thought of Kano's anger. 'I would never do it again to anyone, but at the time it was a way of showing him that I was able to hurt him.'

'I hope that you never have cause to again. We never really liked Kano, Malele.

You were our friend. He wanted to make you his creation as a woman and an artist, and then when Aquilla was born with that arm, he was outraged and could not accept it. He has been transferred to Lagos, I hear, and before he went, he had found another young girl who thought him wonderful.'

'Yes, I think that is true about making me his creation. I was a silly child when I fell in love with him, but he did teach me so much and I owe this exhibition to his teaching, so perhaps it was a good thing in the end. I hope that I can earn a living through art one day.'

Malele went to see Miss Selassie the next day, dressed in one of her smarter salaula dresses. It was good to wear short skirts and shoes with heels again. In the village she had felt out of place in them and had taken to wearing a chitenge cloth over a dress or with a blouse, and flat shoes or flip-flops. Back again in town she was a fairly smart and modern girl, the creation of Kano and her environment. Nancy insisted on taking the case of drawings in the boot of the car.

'Why pay a taxi? I am here and delighted to have something useful to do.

'What happens next?'

'As long as she likes the work, I will have the exhibition. I think she will, as it is better than the ones she saw in the village; the good paper helped a lot and so did the fixative. Everything got so smudged before. Then I have terrible doubts about it.'

'She will. Then?'

'They get framed and a date set for the exhibition. It is to be in the EU building where they have had other exhibitions and Miss Selassie will see to the invitation list and send out the invitations. I don't have to do much except help out on the day before. I can't believe that I am going to have my own exhibition and I have nightmares that she will say the drawings are no good and everything is off.'

Miss Selassie helped her open the wooden case and waited while she held up the charcoal drawings. It was worse than showing them in the village because so much more was at stake. Malele's hand shook. She waited wordlessly as Miss Selassie examined each of them. Nancy was helping by taking them out of the case and handing them to Malele.

'Great. Now let me call the boss. He has the final say, of course, but these are super and I know that he will like them.' She hurried off, leaving Malele and Nancy alone.

'Well done,' Nancy exclaimed. 'I knew she would like them. Stop worrying. Everything is fine.'

Malele didn't answer. Her mouth was dry as she waited for the Head of the European Commission to come and give his verdict. He was a small, fussy man with his spectacles perched far down on his nose. He nodded at the two women and smiled.

'My colleague says the drawings are splendid,' he said. 'Now, hold them up for me. Mine is a strictly untutored eye, but I know what I like and that is something to go by. Thank heavens they are recognizably people, my dear. I have had so many totally unintelligible things through here that this makes a pleasant change. Yes, I like them and they will make an exhibition that is different and should create a lot of interest. Congratulations, my dear. Miss Selassie will make all the arrangements. Mid-morning on a Saturday is the best time for people to come, and the snacks and drinks will be arranged

169

for.' He left them with a slight bow, bustling along the corridor back to his office.

'Right,' said Miss Selassie. 'Now down to the details. Framing will take approximately a week, glass of course, and the invitations should go out soon. Have you people you want to invite, Malele? Just give me a list and I will get them sent, and I will give you one or two for your own distribution. One always forgets someone on the list.'

She was brisk and businesslike. The date was fixed and all Malele had to do was wait impatiently for the great day.

'What are you going to wear?' Nancy asked. 'The artist must look special.'

'I don't know. I still have some of my clothes from when I was here before.

Remember when we went shopping in the salaula market? I had to leave some behind as I could only take a small suitcase that I could carry, and the few art things I packed took up a lot of the space.'

'That was a great day and we had such fun didn't we? How are you off for money? I know that's a rude question, but I have to ask.'

'I have a little left. There are some dollars that I got from Kano. I will turn them into kwacha and we can go shopping for salaula. I can't afford a dress shop.'

'Who can, except the apamwamba. Even on a clinic salary Katele doesn't get all that much. Tomorrow we will go and see what we can find for the occasion. With your shape it will be easy. This is an important occasion and you must have a smart dress.'

The dress she chose had been half hidden under a pile of clothes in a market stall and the glowing flame colour had made Malele pull it out. It was a simple sheath dress, a little crumpled through being packed in a bale of salalua.

'That's from a new bale,' the stallholder said. 'I was going to iron it a bit. It doesn't look so good like that but it has a designer label and it is your size.'

Malele held it against herself. There were no fitting rooms in the salaula market.

'It is my size. What do you think Nancy?'

'You are lucky to find it. It looks good and the colour is perfect. I have a silver pendant that you can borrow as the dress is so plain. You will be the envy of all the women!'

'I would like to think so!' Malele bought the dress and when she got back to Nancy's flat she tried it on.

'Perfect,' Nancy said. 'Not needing any alteration, only an iron. Here is the pendant. Put it on and see for yourself.'

Gazing at her reflection in the long mirror, Malele was satisfied. She would have her hair done, long swept-back extensions, and she had some suitable shoes. She began to feel more confident about the exhibition. At least she would look her best.

Malele was at the exhibition an hour before the first guests were expected. Miss Selassie had suggested this as she said there were sometimes last minute adjustments to the picture hangings to be made, and by being early, Malele could meet the EU staff who would be there. Nancy dropped her off and took Aquilla.

'Let me have him, Malele. I will bring him with me when Katele and I come with the twins, but for now it is better that you don't have to worry about him. This is your big day, remember?'

'As if I could forget. I am so nervous and excited. Thanks, Nancy. I will see you later. Be good, Aquilla.'

'You are looking very smart,' Miss Selassie remarked as they went round checking that the pictures were hanging straight and that there were no smudges on the glass. 'That dress suits you.'

'Salaula. Nancy came with me and helped me to choose.

171

She knows so much more about clothes than I do.'

'Enjoy the exhibition, Malele. I know how nervous you must feel, but most of the people coming will like the work and some will buy if you are lucky. A few come for the occasion and the drink, but most of them are genuine art lovers. I have invited the press and you may get your picture in the papers. All good publicity, and it makes other people come to look, after the opening.'

'You have done so much for me,' Malele said quietly.

'This is something I have dreamed of for a long time, ever since I started to draw and paint. I am grateful to Kano for teaching me even though it was a hard lesson and to you for arranging all this.'

'A pleasure. I always felt bad about the way the gallery treated you when I heard about it. Not that feeling bad would have made me help you if you hadn't been worth helping, but it was so providential finding you at that village school. By the way, how did the kids enjoy the paints? I had an official thank you, but no feedback.'

'They were delighted. It was amazing how they learned to use colour, never having had it before. That was a great kindness on your part.'

'Good. Now, get yourself together and come and stand in the entrance ready to meet the guests. The boss is the official host and wants you there.'

Malele could never remember all that happened at the opening. There were so many people coming and going, shaking her hand and congratulating her on the work. Red sale tickets showed on ten of the pictures and she was in a whirl of excitement.

Petson came in with a small and very sophisticated girl on his arm and they chatted for a few moments. Malele smiled to herself. Trust Petson to have a good-looking partner. He was the same old Petson, and as dear and funny as ever. Then

Boniface came in, alone, more prosperous looking than before, dependent on his sticks. Eunice was not with him and Malele felt disappointed. She had so much wanted all her friends here to see her first solo exhibition.

Boniface came over to where she was standing. She had not seen him since she had fled to the village and there was an air of confidence about him that had not been there before. The lines of pain still pinched his face, but he was more relaxed and outgoing than before.

'Malele, I am so glad to see you. This is such a triumph for you.' He shook her hand, holding it in his gently. 'You are looking wonderful. What a difference to the first time I saw you. You were special then, but now you are even more so.' His eyes held hers and she found him extraordinarily attractive.

'Where is Eunice? I hoped that she would come.'

'No. She decided not to come. She says that she is a village woman in a city and she does not mix with the smart people here.'

'But that is silly.' Jess had said the same thing when they were in the village together.

'No, not silly. Think of bringing your own mother to this sort of gathering ... she would feel out of place and unhappy.

We live in two worlds here, Malele. A traditional one where things are as they have been for centuries, and the one that you and I live in; a more sophisticated one. When you went back to the village you must have understood the difference and being young and educated, you could adapt to either world, but the old cannot. She likes the new flat and all the amenities there, but she sometimes hankers after the old home. That is what she knows best. She will be thinking of you as she sells her food, and wishing you well. She says that she is sorry not to come but that you would understand.'

It was true. Malele hadn't given it a thought until then,

but now she could see what Eunice meant. There were indeed two worlds.

'I do understand. I should have thought. Please give her my love and I will come to see her soon.'

'Have lunch with me when this is over,' Boniface said. 'There is so much to talk about and you have been away for so long. I have passed my last exams and have a good job now, so I can afford it if that is what you were going to say.' He laughed and she joined in, warming to him.

'I would love to. This ends at 1400 hours so there will be no time for lunch, but I would love to have a drink with you somewhere.'

'Fine. We will go to the Garden Court and sit by the pool where it is cool and then we can catch up on the things that have happened. Go and see the rest of your guests and I will find you when the exhibition ends.'

'Wait. I want to show you my son. Nancy has brought him to the exhibition.

There she is over in the corner by the window. You have never seen Aquilla and when we go to the hotel he will stay with Nancy.'

They went over to Katele and Nancy who were talking to a group of people. Malele took Aquilla from her friend and handed him to Boniface. 'This is my son,' she said. 'He has a withered arm, but I hardly notice it.' For some reason she wanted him to know.

'Eunice told me. A pity, but it will be a small handicap. I, too, have come to terms with mine and so will he. He is a fine child.'

Aquilla reached up to touch Boniface's hair. The man took the twisted arm in his hand and smiled.

Chapter 19

The aftermath of the exhibition lacked excitement. Not that Malele had expected anything amazing to happen but somehow there was an anti-climax. A few days after the opening, Boniface handed her a newspaper.

ARTIST SHOWS PORTRAITS AT EU EXHIBITION

On Saturday an exhibition of charcoal portraits was opened at the EU Headquarters in Lusaka. Local artist Malele Simonga showed a rare talent for portraiture in a series of studies. One of the most powerful drawings is entitled "Ambuya". The artist tells me that this is a portrait of her grandmother which she did in the village. The choice of medium is both unusual and effective and the public showed its approval by buying most of the twenty-five works on display. We understand that Miss Simonga has been offered sponsorship to study in Britain for a year and we look forward to her next exhibition on her return.

'The paper has an account of the exhibition,' Boniface remarked. The paper was two days old and he was sure that she had seen it. 'I didn't know that you were going to Britain.'

'I wasn't sure. I still don't know officially and I didn't want to tell you and Eunice until I was certain.'

Boniface moved restlessly. 'You won't come back. There have been many artists who have gone overseas and have decided to stay where there is more opportunity.'

'I will come back. This is home and all my family and friends are here.'

'Perhaps.'

'No, really I will. If everything goes all right I will go to the college and after that I will be back to find a job here. I hope that I will get one with some publishing firm, and then I can get Aquilla back from my mother and make arrangements for him to be looked after in working hours.'

'Aquilla will be a village child by then.'

'Maybe, but he will have lots of love and care until I return.' Malele put her hand on Boniface's shoulder. 'I will miss all of you, especially Aquilla, but in the end it will be worthwhile. Write to me, Boniface, and give me all the news.'

He nodded and slid his hand over hers. For a moment she thought that he would kiss her and she was torn between longing for his love and fear at starting another relationship. Boniface let her hand go and turned away.

'A year is a long time. My mother and I will be waiting for you.' The flash of intimacy was gone and they were again friends who had nothing between them.

In the days before Malele left for Britain she took the child back to the village. Jess was waiting, eager to have Aquilla, and Esnart marvelled over him and how big he was getting.

'Another year and he will be a boy and not a baby,' she said.

'He will be loved here, Malele, and when you come back he will be waiting. I am glad for you to have this opportunity. I feel proud that I have helped towards it, even in a small way.' She kissed Malele gently.

'I may not see you again, my child, but remember that I wish you well and every success.'

'Of course I will see you again, ambuya. I am only away for a year.'

Malele held the old, blind woman closely, but she, too, felt that perhaps this was the final parting. She brushed the premonition aside. She was leaving the village early in the morning and Aquilla would stay there. Jess had softened and she knew that the child would be well cared for.

There was so much to do before she left. Nancy insisted on taking her to the airport and there she found Boniface and Eunice with Petson, all grouped together to say goodbye. For a moment Malele was tempted to cancel her trip and stay with her friends, but so much had been arranged that she felt that she had to go.

'I will write,' said Boniface as he kissed her goodbye. 'See you in a year.'

Malele was tempted to fling her arms around him, but his kiss was casual and gave her no encouragement. She turned away and said goodbye to the others, then went up the staircase to the departure lounge. The image of Boniface remained with her and she did not know whether to be glad or sorry that he appeared to have no romantic feelings for her.

London was grey and damp when she arrived. The UN had found her accommodation near the college and the representative took her there. The room was small and shabby and, once alone, Malele burst into tears of homesickness. She wasn't sure what she had expected, but in this grey city she was a stranger and very insignificant. The people who had met her at the airport were friendly enough, but it was an official friendliness, meeting a student who had been given a grant. She wished that some familiar face would appear and that she could find a friend already here, but there was no one. She pulled the bedclothes over her head and dreamed of Africa.

The next morning she was introduced to the college and to the tutors and her life as a student began. Soon she was part of the college life, but always there remained a deeply felt longing to be in Africa together with her child. She thought of Boniface too and the sight of anyone wearing callipers recalled him vividly. He wrote often, casual letters giving her all the local news and sending messages from Eunice. Nancy wrote too, and there were a few letters from the village, written by someone Jess knew and dictated to, giving news of Aquilla.

Malele poured over them, shedding tears as she thought of her child and her friends, but in the end the homesickness wore off. She began to share in the student life and enjoy her studies, knowing that time was passing and the year would soon be up. She found that she was one of the better students and occasionally was singled out for praise by the tutors, but mainly she simply worked hard and tried to prepare herself for her return.

She was an attractive woman and after several mild flirtations with fellow students, which never got beyond the banter stage, Malele found herself attracted by a tutor who was in charge of the life study class. He had brilliant grey eyes and thinning hair. From the start he showed an interest in her work and Malele found herself warming to him. At first it was the relationship of a student to an experienced and influential teacher, but Malele gradually found herself thinking about him as a man who was attractive and exciting. For weeks he was a nagging excitement, then one day John Callaghan asked her if she would have supper with him at a nearby restaurant. The invitation came at an opportune time for Malele had just received a letter from the village telling her that Esnart had died peacefully in her sleep and that she had been buried in the village cemetery. The news upset her although she had wondered if she would ever see her grandmother again when she left. Esnart had been such a powerful influence on her that Malele felt a great void in her life. The prospect of an evening out with someone she admired was tempting.

'I thought that we would try the place round the corner. It's unpretentious but I hear that the food is good. You aren't a vegetarian are you?' She shook her head.

'Thanks. I'd like that.'

She was already planning what she should wear, and she felt excited at the prospect of the meal. It had been a long time since she had felt like this and as Boniface's letters showed no more than a casual interest, there was no reason not to enjoy herself. Grieving for Esnart would not bring her back. She met him outside the restaurant and together they pushed through the bead curtains and into the room. She followed him to a table near the window. He pulled out her chair in a display of old-fashioned gallantry which surprised her and made her smile. Few of her contemporaries would have done that, there was a more aggressive equality between the sexes.

'Thanks.'

They ordered from the plastic-sheeted menu and a harassed waiter filled their wine glasses with the cheap house wine. Conversation was easy and pleasant and they had the college in common. Malele relaxed and felt the wine coursing through her body. He was attractive. The subdued light hid his thinning hair and the candle light reflected in his eyes. She wondered how he would make love, whether he was a good lover or whether he would be stiff and inhibited. She had never been to bed with anyone except Kano and tonight she was almost prepared to try. It had been a long time since Kano had roused her.

'I wanted to find out whether you were interested in working here after the course has ended, Malele. A friend of mine has a vacancy for an artist and I wondered if you would be interested?'

Malele was jolted from her sensual reveries. This man was strictly impersonal.

For a moment she was disappointed, then she was glad and shocked at her imaginings. How could she have even thought of such things, but it was a sign that she had got over Kano and was ready to live again.

'I am going back home in two months so there is no question of working here,' she said firmly. She would see Boniface again and all her friends. 'Thank you for thinking of me, but I need to go home. I have a small child there. He is with my mother at present, but once I have found work I will get him from the village.'

The man seemed interested in her life in Zambia and she found herself telling him about her affair with Kano and how her life had changed. Malele knew that the wine had loosened her tongue, but as she would be leaving London soon it did not seem to matter. She would probably never see her tutor again and she did owe him an explanation for refusing the job. He was charming and interested, and in return he told her a little about how he had never married as the girl had died before the wedding and he had never found anyone else. It was an exchange that surprised both of them, but it did not matter. The next day things were back to normal and Malele enjoyed his life class without any sensual thoughts about him.

The year passed quickly and it was time to catch the flight back to Lusaka. She would spend a day or two in Lusaka, then take the bus to the village and collect Aquilla. After that she would look for a job, for the grant had ended after a year. Malele had written to Nancy giving the time of arrival and as she came out of the customs area, there was Nancy waving and smiling to her.

'Lovely to have you back,' Nancy cried as they hugged one another, then together they pushed the laden trolly out of the concourse.

'Your room is waiting for you. Tomorrow we are having a dinner for you and I have invited Boniface and Petson. Boniface has been like a lost soul since you left and only cheered up when he knew you were actually coming back. I think he feared that you would stay in the UK.'

'Rubbish. He did write, but they certainly weren't exciting letters. He has no real interest in me.'

Nancy laughed. 'Stick to your story girl. I can assure you that he is in love.'

Malele felt her heart leap at the news. His letters had been so casual and there had been no sense of his missing her. For her part she knew that Boniface was a part of her life and she was afraid that her feelings for him were not reciprocated. Now there seemed hope that he had really missed her. Thank goodness she had waited for him, but he had made no move in her direction and all the affection seemed to be on her side.

The dinner party brought her oldest friends together, all except Eunice who had stayed at home, saying that it was a young people's party. Nancy and her husband had invited Petson and Boniface but that was all.

Malele dressed with care for the event, glad that she had shed the extra pounds that had accumulated at the beginning of her stay in London. The sheath dress with its low-cut neckline made her look exotic and she hoped that Boniface would notice. Perhaps Nancy was right and he was in love with her, but she could not find any signs of it. For her part, he was familiar and dear and she was in love with him. Petson was part of her life too, but only as a friend.

The evening wore on and Malele tried to see some sign of unrequited passion in Boniface, but there was none and he was his usual charming self. In desperation she flirted with Petson who entered into the spirit of things light-heartedly.

'Boniface certainly isn't in love with me,' Malele said flatly as she and Nancy discussed the party next morning. 'You must have imagined it.'

Nancy laughed. 'No, I am right. Give him time and trust me! I am sure that he doesn't want to rush you and he knows that he is disabled so that makes him hang back. Has he any hope?' She was suddenly serious.

Malele thought for a moment to make sure of what she was saying.

'I love him, Nancy. It took time to get over Kano and all that has happened, but a year away has made me certain.'

'Patience, girl, patience. Things will come right you'll see.'

Malele took the bus to the village the next day. She had intended to find a job and accommodation first, but she was impatient to reclaim her child. After all her travels, it looked small and shabby but achingly familiar. Aquilla hardly knew her and this upset Malele.

'He is a real village child and doesn't even know who I am,' she complained as he went back to Jess's side after she had hugged the reluctant boy. 'He is looking well but he thinks I am a sort of stranger.'

'Well you have been away for over a year and he is very young.' Jess was unsympathetic. 'I hope it was worth it and that you are staying at home now, not gadding off to foreign places and leaving the child. Not that I mind having him. He is very dear to me, but he needs a mother who will stay put.'

Malele hung her head. Jess was right, but deep down she knew that she had been right to go to the college and that in the end she would benefit from the experience. Now she must re-establish her relationship with Aquilla - and start one with Boniface if that was possible. Before she left the village she went to the cemetery to say goodbye to Esnart. The grave was one of the newer ones, still marked with the rawness of the earth, but beginning to be softened by the creeping kapinga grass. It was very quiet and shaded by trees which threw their shadows over the old graves. Malele shivered. Ambuya seemed very close.

'Goodbye ambuya. You were right when you said that you wouldn't see me when I came back. Thank you for everything.'

The tears spilled over her cheeks. She missed her grandmother and the village wasn't the same without her, despite the warm welcome that she had had. The school was just the same as when she had taught art there, and even Zulu had greeted her, showing off his new baby, but things were different. 'Ambuya was the centre of my life here,' Malele thought. 'Now that she has gone there is nothing to keep me here, not even my mother. I have moved on to the city and that is my home.'

Returning to Lusaka with Aquilla she found a day crèche that took small children and enrolled him there. Then she began searching for a job.

Armed with her experience and the certificate from the college, she soon found a place with a publisher, illustrating textbooks and stories. In her spare time she could do her own work and the small flat that went with the job would provide accommodation for the two of them. She moved out from Nancy's flat and into her own. Aquilla cried when he left Jess, but he soon forgot the village life and began to accept Malele as the most important person in his life. He would greet Eunice and Boniface as well as the other friends who came to the flat, waving in welcome.

'He is a bright child,' Eunice said one day as the two women sat together.

'I love him like my own. And so does Boniface.' She looked hard at Malele. 'Is there nothing between you two? I have no right to ask, but as I am like your grandmother I am curious. I had hoped that you would become fond of each other and when you went off, I noticed how Boniface grieved in private. I knew because I am his mother and we live together. Now that you are back he is withdrawn and tense.'

'I wish I knew. I love him, but as you say he gives me no encouragement and he is only a casual friend.'

'Do you really love him? He is very crippled, but he is clever and loving and has a great future. I say this as a proud mother.'

'I do love him. I do. So does Aquilla.'

'Well, there is little that we can do. He will make up his own mind, but I would be so happy to see you together. A wise woman can encourage a man, even one as shy as my son and that is the only advice I can offer you.'

183

Malele thought over the advice. Perhaps Boniface didn't love her, but both Nancy and Eunice seemed certain that he did. She decided that she must be the one to make the running and if she failed at least she would have tried. It was better to know.

She invited him to dinner alone, and spent hours preparing his favourite food. She was a moderate cook and there were some disasters. The tomato sauce was scorched and had to be thrown out and a fresh lot made, the pudding didn't set until she had remembered to add gelatine, but in the end she managed. The table was set western style for she had become used to this and she knew that Boniface liked the formality of dining this way. She placed candles and flowers on the table.

'I wish that I had a record player,' she thought. 'Romantic music would help!'

She spent a long time over her appearance and by the time the doorbell rang she was ready. Boniface arrived and Malele greeted him at the door. 'Come in, Boniface. Aquilla wants to say goodnight to you before he goes off to bed. He was determined to see you.'

She was talking too much and the conversation sounded false. With Aquilla in bed, they were alone and for some reason, both were ill at ease.

'All your favourites' she said as they started the meal.
He ate some of the food, but for once his appetite seemed poor and Malele was concerned. She wondered if the meal was badly cooked.

'You have hardly eaten,' she said. 'Are you all right?'

'Perfectly. You haven't eaten much either.'

'I'm not hungry. Preparing the food has ruined my appetite. Not that I am a great cook.'

'I am sure that you are. This meal is very good.'

It sounded trite. They sat in candlelit silence. The clock on the wall ticked off the seconds with maddening precision. Malele started to speak and so did Boniface and suddenly the ridiculous humour of the situation made them both burst out laughing.

'We are sitting here like two idiots,' Boniface said. He was quiet for a moment, his eyes searching her face. 'I came here to ask you to marry me and everything has gone wrong. I have wanted to ask you since before you went to Britain, but I didn't want to hold you back from having a good time if you wanted to. Then I thought that maybe you would stay there and not come back.'

'I was always coming back and I wish that you had asked me. Your letters were so casual that I wondered if you cared at all, and when I got back you didn't seem to care that much.'

'Of course I cared, but marrying a cripple is hardly something I can expect you to do, but I now have to ask.'

'I love you, Boniface, and the overseas trip made me see how much I missed you.'

They were together and his face was close to hers. 'You will marry me won't you Malele? I can take care of you and Aquilla. He needs a father and I need a son. Now that I am part of a big firm I earn a good salary.'

'Yes, oh yes. I have wanted this to happen for so long, and I wondered if it ever would.'

They planned the wedding together, but it was Malele who really took charge and Boniface let her make the decisions.

'I want a quiet family and close friends wedding in a church,' Malele said. 'Not a village one as I have been away too long and have grown apart from the traditional feast. My mother and Uncle Silas will have to come here as our guests for the wedding. We can arrange all that when we go to the village to meet them. They will come briefly, but they will want to return to their village life where they are happy.'

She smiled at Boniface. 'You are a townie too. Is that all right?'

'Whatever you want. I suppose that I will have to ask

your uncle for you? That part of tradition is still essential, and I will have to meet your mother. Have you a bride price?'

Malele laughed. 'Probably Uncle Silas expects one. He respects tradition, especially where money is involved. He had to repay the original one and that rankled. My mother will be delighted that her wayward daughter is at last getting a respectable and wage-earning husband. Your mother is no problem and we are as close as if she was my real mother.'

'So there are no problems. Oh Malele. This has made me so happy. I was so afraid that you would turn me down.'

'I waited long enough.'

She didn't tell him that she had made up her mind to make the running. Let him think that it was all his idea. She pictured the future with Boniface. One day there would be several small half brothers and sisters for Aquilla to play with. She would go on painting and perhaps become famous, but the main thing was that she and Boniface would have a life together. Eunice would live with them and could continue her selling as long as she wished. The future stretched happily before them.

They were married in July and spent a week in Kariba on their honeymoon. It was a time of great joy and tenderness for both of them. Eunice took care of Aquilla who had grown to love his new ambuya, and this time the boy was waiting to welcome them home.

Petson came to call when they returned and handed Malele a cutting from a local newspaper that had come out while they were away. Malele pasted it into her scrapbook. As Boniface remarked, it did give the bare essentials of the event, but the joy and excitement stayed with the Phiris.

WEDDING BELLS FOR A LOCAL ARTIST

The happy couple pictured in today's newspaper show the former Miss Malele Simonga and Mr Boniface Phiri after their marriage in St Ignatius Church. The bride is a well-known artist who recently completed her sponsored studies at a British art college and the groom is with an accountancy firm in Lusaka.

'The bare essentials,' said Boniface. 'Come on Mrs Phiri, we will be late for work and we still have to drop Aquilla off at the crèche.'

She closed the scrapbook. Some day, when both she and Boniface were old, they would relive their lives through the scrapbook, and their children would know how their lives had changed over time. It would be a record of their history and Malele would have recorded all the important happenings over the years. She smiled and went out to the waiting car.

The end

Printed in the United States
By Bookmasters